# Cry Havoc

*Paul R. Starling*

*Copyright*
*Paul R Starling*
*Contact: p.starling@sky.com*

*Front cover artwork, design and layout*
*Chloe Starling*

*First Edition 2024*

*All rights reserved. No part of this publication may be reproduced, stored in a retrieval system, or transmitted in any form or by any means, electronic, mechanical, photocopy, recording or otherwise, without prior written permission from the copyright holder. Nor can it be circulated in any form of binding or cover other than that in which it is published and without similar condition being imposed on a similar purchaser.*

Thank you to Andrew for your support on this venture.

This book is dedicated with sincere thanks
to all my readers…and Sooty.

# CHAPTER ONE

Alfie Ross was on the phone to his father and his hands were sweating anxiously. Not solely because of his father's political prominence and his privileged family status, Alfie had gotten used to that as a young man all those years ago. This was different. His new anxiety had been caused by the Private Investigator and all the questions the man had asked. What bordered on an interrogation had worried Alfie, gnawed at his subconscious and the worry had privately transformed into anger, twisting his gut, spoiling his appetite, and Alfie enjoyed his food.

"Now Winston, my boy," Lambert Ross said. "Does this impact our schedule?"

His fathers deep voice remained at an even cadence but Alfie know differently. And so he should. His father had been a politician. Still thought of himself as one, the aspirations dormant. Alfie could read between his fathers unspoken lines.

"No." Alfie was confident it didn't affect any schedule which they had previously discussed.

"And you remained calm?"

"Yes."

"At all times?"

"Yes."

"What did the investigator ask?"

"Oh, just questions about work." Alfie said, trying to downplay the situation. His mind was a maelstrom of emotions, unusually for him, and the words tumbled rapidly out of his mouth. "He asked what I do at the facility. The nature of the facility itself. Who I work with. Do I associate with colleagues socially. What do I think of my boss!"

"Did he ask about me?"

"Of course he did. I'm your son."

"What did he ask?"

"Nothing, really."

"Winston!"

Alfie hated his birth name. His father was the only one who called him Winston. Named after the great Prime Minister of England, of course. Alfie's father was extremely patriotic and believed there was no name or person more synonymous with Great Britain than Winston Churchill. Thankfully his mother had chosen the middle name Alfred, which was much more preferable and Alfie's choice had been one of the main reasons he and his father fell out. Plus, Alfie blamed his father for his mother's death, hence the underlying animosity.

"The investigator knew we had fallen out years ago." Alfie said. "But I told him I hadn't spoken to you in years, which is mostly true. I think he was just- probing. Looking for a bit of gossip, or something, I don't know, but it's all fine."

"You're certain?"

"Yes."

"Okay, Winston. I believe you."

Alfie reined in his anger. He knew a political lie. His father had never truly believed in anything his son had done, even when he had earned a double PHD in the sciences. Alfie's father had continually brushed him aside like he didn't matter to the family name. And yet now his father significantly required his ability.

"How is the project?" Lambert Ross asked convivially, like the best politician putting on the fake charm.

"I told you it's on schedule."

"Okay, fine. And how are you?"

"What do you care?" Alfie snorted derisively.

"I don't. But you are my son and I want to be proud of you, so stop acting like the spoiled brat you used to be and join the adult world. I would think a couple of phd's might've made a man out of you, but clearly not."

"Well, once this is over and you've paid me in full you'll be pleased to know I shall be out of your life." Alfie's anger was roiling upon the point of pathetic tears of emotion, which definitely wouldn't do. His father always did like to humiliate his son, and if not for the huge sum of money which would set Alfie up for the remainder of his life, he would tell the man where to go using the most colourful metaphors he could conjure. He wanted to end the call, but Alfie was not going to be the first to hang up the phone. "How's your new wife?"

"Berenice is doing well, thank you,"

"Good."

"Who are you getting to initiate the plan?"

"The friend I told you about already."

"Oh yes, the char lady ." Lambert Ross said, using the descriptive disdainfully. "And she thinks she's doing it for the betterment of mankind?"

"She is, isn't she?"

"No need to be facetious, Winston."

"She believes her task is being done to restore family values and the spirit of the community." Alfie intoned as if quoting a manifesto.

"As well she is."

"And your political ambitions."

"Does she know that?"

"Of course not." Alfie scoffed. "She would not go ahead with the job if she believed it was purely to foster your aspirations."

"Good." Lambert Ross said. "Goodbye, Winston."

"Goodbye, sir."

The line went dead. Alfie grinned at the irony as he too hung up. The relationship between him and his father had died years ago.

Alfie poured himself a drink. His only vice. That and the Norwich nightclub he visited, which might be on the cards tonight to rid himself of the bitter aftertaste of his chat with his father. That was something between him and the like minded men he met there, although father probably already knew about that particular proclivity. Alfie had certainty borne the brunt of his father's narrow mindedness on numerous occasions in his youth, such was the older man's staid attitude. Lambert Ross had even paid a woman to pleasure his then sixteen year old son, but that had scarred him more deeply. Those days were far behind him.

Alfie sat and drank, despair becoming a looming cloud in his mind. A devious whirlwind of thoughts consumed him, and a plot developed whose narrative would culminate in murder if he got his wish!

## CHAPTER TWO

Political correctness be damned because Harry Kovac was unashamedly staring in appreciation of the female form which cruised a foot below the surface of the swimming pool. Parisa Dane was naked and an exceptionally fine sight to behold. Harry thought himself a very fortunate fellow indeed. They had been a couple for over twelve-months now and the newness to their relationship hadn't waned, the spark of excitement which kept them moving ever forward remained present. He smiled inwardly at the thought that he was almost forty years old and acting like an adolescent.

Also it wouldn't exactly dampen a person's spirits that their surroundings were truly idyllic.

It was a late summer afternoon and the sunshine topped the trees which surround Villa d'Remy in the French Dordogne. More precisely the villa was part of a trio nestled amongst poplars along the Route Du Theil in Vitrac, situated in an easterly direction from the nearby large and popular commune and tourist destination Sarlat-la-Caneda.

The villa was positioned in the lower basin of a valley and offered peaceful tranquility without being far from the beaten track. The property consisted of a large double garage at the end of a gravel turning square, a gated entrance, with the main two-storey villa to the right of this, concealing the garden and patio area from the road. The unimpressive oblong building was painted ochre with brown window frames and catered comfortably for eight guests - Harry and Parisa had been remarkably fortunate that the owners had had a cancellation, and with Harry's employer being flush with cash, money was no object when it came to finding this property. Out back was a neatly cut lawn bordered by blooming flower beds, a stone barbecue up one end and a ping-pong table the other. A large wooden table and chairs set rested upon the concrete patio, and to the rear of the lawn on a manmade raised area was the generously proportioned swimming pool.

Parisa emerged from the water which cascaded off her skin and silken hair that she casually slicked back from her face, and padded toward Harry. He handed her a glass of locally produced wine they had purchased in Sarlat the day before.

"Cheers." Parisa said and took a drink. Droplets of condensation dripped off the glass where it had been in the iced bucket before Harry had filled it, running down the centre of her body, before she said at length: "This is the life."

Harry could not, and would not, disagree. They were being paid to be here by Stephen Smith, an eccentric English businessman whose flair for adventure, and desire for celebrity, saw Harry, employee of Crane Investigation Services - a small private investigation firm based in Norfolk, England - on a quest to recover a long-missing automobile. Smith paid well mainly because, twelve months previously, a successful assignment had thrust him in the limelight and he wanted to continue his public image with something similar. Harry wasn't enamoured with Smith or his associate, Climmy, but the investigation firm had most certainly benefited from this exposure, and business was subsequently booming.

Parisa downed her wine and sat on a lounger beside Harry, letting the air and sunshine dry her.

"I think I should invest in a villa like this." Parisa said. She was a property agent whose business was also booming thanks to receptive clients who rightly trusted her successes and advice. "I mean for us. We could rent it out when we aren't using it. This could be our home away from home."

"You won't get any objection from me." Harry agreed, and refilled their wine glasses. "Especially as the wine is perfect in this region."

Parisa raised her glass, and said with a wry smile: "Cheers to your friends Stephen Smith and what's the other guys name, the one you really like?"

Harry rolled his eyes. Smith and Climmy certainly weren't his friends. Smith was a shark-eyed mute who was unreadable and totally unresponsive as a human; while Climmy was an over exuberant Londoner with an assortment of irritating phrases and quirks whose lights required punching out but, being a client, Harry had to grit his teeth whilst in the man's presence.

"They are paying the bills, I suppose." Harry offered somewhat grudgingly.

"And it's exciting. I'm pleased you brought me along. We could be the first to answer a quarter-century old mystery."

"It's just a car." Harry said glibly.

"Oh, don't be a boring old fart! It's not just any car. It's James Bonds Aston Martin DB5!"

"Like I said: it's just a car."

"It's not just a car."

"Okay, it's a historically significant car to those with nothing better than pay exorbitant amounts of money for such memorabilia. We are on a high adventure at the behest of a self-promoting, self-loving glory hunter, who hopes that we can succeed were many others, professionals amongst them, mind you, have failed. But it's still only a car!"

"It's exciting. A quest of passion. Your name will be etched in the annals of history."

Harry laughed at Parisa's clear over the top attempt to rile him. He enjoyed the banter. Parisa took pleasure in mocking his total lack of consumer desires. She was younger than him and retained much more youthful thoughts and desires. Since this assignment had landed in Harry's lap, they had discussed the often ludicrous sums of money paid out for trinkets which were often only significant to the buyer, and the greed of the seller. Trinkets of the idle rich, who were most of Parisa's customer base. Since receiving this assignment Harry had indeed learned much about the automotive industry and the car collectors with their passions which were fuelled on account of a wide range of reasons. But it didn't alter his perception of cars: they were for getting from A to B and back again. And that's it!

"That'll be lovely."

Parisa stood and stretched languidly, before she straddled him and sat upon his hips.

"At least there are some things you are passionate about."

Arching forward she rested her chest on his. They kissed and Harry's smartphone rang. He ignored it but it was insistent upon his attention. The caller rang off and they continued their love-making until once more the phone rang.

"Bloody technology." Harry said.

"You could try turning it off." Parisa offered, sitting upright, fingers tracing lines down his chest. She giggled playfully. "Turning you on, sir!"

"Usually it's your phone that disturbs my concentration!" Harry said wryly, and reluctantly scooped up the phone, wishing he had indeed either left the phone in the villa, or switched it off entirely.

The caller display told Harry that it was Daphne Crane, the unspoken head of Crane Investigation Services who, along with her husband Zero, had founded the organisation. Harry answered, his face dropping as he listened to what he was being told.

"Okay." Harry said into the smartphone, voice wavering as he tried to absorb what he had just heard. "Hang tight, Daphne. We will be home as soon as we can."

Harry disconnected the call.

"What's wrong?" Parisa asked him.

"Zero has been in an accident." Harry said plainly. "He's dead."

# CHAPTER THREE

"Heads or tails?" Asked Zero Crane while passing a silver coin between his fingers.

A coin toss had become the traditional way in which he and Harry Kovac decided who took what case if two presented themselves simultaneously, although in one weeks time this system will have to be rethought when a third member would be joining their team.

Expansion of the firm had become inevitable. Business was booming because of their association with Stephen Smith and the publicity surrounding their treasure hunting job for him, and the final outcome of that assignment, which Harry had spearheaded. Crane Investigation Services had 'and Associate' attached to its name now, making the partnership team more official, recognising Harry's importance. Their office was situated along Magdalen Street, Norwich, accessed through a gated entrance and had been there since the firms inception, with Daphne Crane the first face which new clients saw.

Work had flooded in like never before, with no word-of-mouth or expensive advertising necessary to promote them. Still, the vast majority of their bread and butter business remained a constant: philandering partners. Men, women and gender fluid who believed their significant other needed investigation for whatever reason were the firms staple job. It was a timeworn story of betrayal or suspicion or both and more, on some level, which technology had rendered more or less, depending upon one's point of view, sophisticated.

Hence the newly appointed addition, Teri Hamilton, who would officially start next week. Fresh out of the Metropolitan Police Department, Teri had moved to

Norfolk seeking a change of lifestyle direction - similar in many ways to Harry's decision. She was successful at the job but became disenchanted by the political dynamics and power struggles inherent within certain organisations, deciding that a new career path was a desirable option. Again, this was a very similar path taken up by Harry, who knew how long ago.

Harry and Zero had reached the hypothesis many years in their past that society had gone to the dogs with no sign of a turnaround on the horizon. As long as humans existed on planet Earth there would always be a need for criminal investigation services and funeral parlours! That was their conclusion.

The coin toss involved two cases which could literally be called opposite sides of the coin.

Firstly, or heads, would be a return to the employ of Stephen Smith and Climmy. As explained over the phone to Daphne by the over-the-top exuberant and excitable nature of Climmy, bordering on the edge of irritation, the dubious duo had purchased an abandoned farmhouse. With it came a car collection that was bequeathed them by their ownership. Their representative in the purchase had discovered an item that might very well lead them to unearth a two decades old mystery surrounding a missing automobile. Climmy had not been willing to announce over the phone which significant automobile might be involved, but clearly his tone of intrigue and gravitas coupled with excitement had been aimed at building some level of suspense.

Secondly, and the tails side of the coin was a case which on its surface seemed like nothing more than sifting through a mound of personnel records and data. The only real interesting notion was that their employer was a sophisticated and relatively secret research and development firm on the outskirts of Norwich, trading under the innocuous name of Carlson & Whimpole. When Daphne had accepted the job on the firms behalf she had asked what it was that the company researched and developed, but the reply was vague, a non-committal committee appointed response about scientific government projects, which could mean anything from technology, weaponry or even biological research. All they wanted the Crane firm to do was their annual staff security appraisal, independently verified, which mostly meant paperwork, but occasionally there was a requirement for face to face meetings if anything out of the ordinary presented itself.

"Reluctantly," Harry said, "I shall opt for heads. But only because it sounds less like boring paperwork."

"LOL!" Zero acknowledged deadpan before he laughed out loud anyway.

"I hate doing it to you!"

"If it comes up tails, I'm delegating the boring job to you."

"Fair enough, boss."

Harry had done his share of these mundane cases in his time with the firm, in fact employers wishing to vet their employees had become a staple business for them, much like the aforementioned cheating. There were too many people illegally placed in English society these days for employers of any description to risk unwanted bad publicity. These jobs were not followed up by the firm, it was solely in the hands of the employer to act on the data gathered.

Rarely did the firm venture into jobs which the police handled themselves, although after a local murder investigation where the accused man's wife had pleaded on

Harry's doorstep for help, and its subsequent successful outcome - at least the press had claimed it had been a success, despite the man's subsequent death at the hands of a local thug, and the wife's psychological trauma - they had naturally received similar pleas. But usually these were not the modern crime investigation firms domain, too much forties gumshoe under the bridge!

The coin once tossed hung tantalisingly in the air for less than a split-second before returning in its descent to land in Zero's hand, the Kings head enigmatically announcing the outcome.

"For goodness sake!" Zero said with facepalm resignation.

"Sorry, boss."

"But I like cars."

"And I dislike cars and the client, so really whose the loser?"

"Sure you don't want to swap?"

After a brief pretend hesitation Harry shrugged his shoulders apologetically.

Daphne came into the open doorway at that exact moment like she had heard the exchange, which she probably had because there were no secrets within the office.

"You are expected at eleven." She told Harry, then, to Zero: "Our solicitor is on the phone."

Zero visibly slumped in his seat as if somebody had pressed down upon his shoulders. "Okay. Thanks."

Presently the firm were faced with a client who was suing them for mis-representation of her instructions going back nearly six months. Another thing which success attracted were money grubbing people who saw an opportunity for self-publicity, with too much time on their hands and anger in their soul. This client had come to them with a case which they took in good faith and when they carried out the job that faith backfired. The moral being that the investigator should do his or her job properly when vetting all clients! This was a mistake that could be costly, and one which they wouldn't repeat.

Harry waved himself out of the office, no more words needed to be spoken.

# CHAPTER FOUR

"My friend!" Climmy practically shouted the greeting, grinning widely and extending his arms wider. Harry Kovac wasn't a joyless wonder but this little man's voice, his patter, his very posture and garishly bright clothing, were just filled with over-the-top fakery. Harry was a realistic man capable of dissecting bravado and bluster, plus a person comfortable with telling everyone that they are their friend clearly had personality issues.

"Good morning." Harry said with undisguised boredom laced in his voice, noting that this annoying man was sweating profusely and his face shone from the gleam of light.

Stephen Smith stood behind Climmy and was the complete polar opposite to his companion. Smith wore a pale suit, was stoically focused and lacked any kind of empathy. Trying to equal Smith's stare with one of his own was impossible to maintain. The man's fateful existence had rendered him fully incapable of emotion, stunted his expression, while physically altering his countenance. He was a shell of humanity, dead-eyed, but his powerfully active brain had created great financial success.

Harry noted with little interest that the Norwich apartment was evidently going through a phase of complete refurbishment. Gone were the bank of LED screens that had covered a wall to present an exotic view of choice. The wall behind was far less interesting. The corner bar with its once elaborate coffee machine was half dismantled, while the remaining furniture was covered in tarpaulins.

Harry cared not but Climmy took it upon himself to explain that the screens were being replaced by far higher resolution technology, the latest, apparently, and the bar was being turned into some glass and steel contraption designed by someone who Harry had never heard of, while a bespoke manufacturer was creating a coffee machine specifically to Climmy's specifications.

One certainly didn't require the mind of a detective to realise this meeting was taking place somewhere other than the apartment. The duo were now heading toward the elevator.

"We're heading out, Amigo." Climmy announced with unnecessary exposition. "There's this little cafe, best in the City, which serves an awesome Americano. Obviously we can't talk here. Construction workers arriving in ten minutes. That okay, my friend?"

Harry nodded and followed them. The elevator moved imperceptibly downward. The duo exchanged pleasantries with the doorman slash security guard, and they were out into the morning City pedestrians.

Climmy enthusiastically spun small talk about he and Smith's escapades, to which Harry grunted the odd acknowledgment when he deemed such was required. Inwardly, Harry was practising a mental calming mantra which Parisa Dane had taught him that had worked wonders for their sex life, but was equally effective for enabling self-control when it came to urges to physically punching to a stop Climmy's verbal diarrhoea. Harry also reminded himself that these were well-paying clients of the investigation service who he was now an associate of, despite their intolerable characteristics.

In a grandiose yet gentlemanly gesture, Climmy held open the glass door by its vertical metal bar for both Smith and Harry when they reached the cafe which, by appearances alone, looked like any other fashionably expensive coffee house. This did have something positive to offer though because it wasn't a franchised name that Harry had heard of.

The interior smell was amazing. Coffee and sweet pastries. An irresistible combination to the senses.

After familial bantering and the ordering of the overpriced and pretentiously named beverages from the abundance of variations on offer, plus a plateful of breakfast pastries, the trio took a table behind the front window. Harry sat with his back to wall out of habit, facing his surroundings. The motif of the establishment was modern art which created a sense of depth, angled planes and multi-surface collages. Harry was no art expert but could certainly appreciate the effective synergy of the style within the relatively narrow, oblong room. The idea was probably a counterpoint to the effects of excessive caffeine.

"Whaddaya know, my friend?" Climmy asked, probably feeling he had dominated the conversation thus far, although the phrase was one from his stock repertoire when he had nothing of real substance to say!

"What do you have for us this time?" Harry asked with interest, looking politely from Smith firstly, who couldn't answer, then to Climmy.

Climmy's eyes lit up and he immediately commenced with an excited oration: "Four weeks ago Stephen and me came upon a bargain property for sale in Roughton." Climmy referred to a widely dispersed village straddling the A140 twenty miles north of Norwich, four miles south of coastal town Cromer. "This farmhouse from the nineteen thirties and its land was being auctioned off by Addy-Benton. There's woodlands and farm fields surrounding this forty-acre estate which at one time must've been a cash cow for its owner. Now it's dilapidated and overgrown. The owner died three years ago. It's taken this long for it to come on the market. But this guy was a rich recluse, big in Boston. That's America, not Lincolnshire!" He laughed as his own joke but when nobody joined in, he continued: "He was in the automotive industry, moved to normal Norfolk twenty-five years ago with no family or friends and a disability which eventually limited his mobility. Are you with me?" Climmy briefly paused for breath. "This guy severed ties with the States utterly, and I mean totally! We found out a few facts ourselves, Stephen and me. Addy-Benton had the bare details on the property." Climmy looked to Smith. "Guy's business was right next door to our hotel in Boston. Who knew?"

"Do you employ Russian assassins at that one, also?" Harry asked deadpan. He was alluding to the controversy surrounding their Norwich country club Beeston Grange. It had been here that a particularly nasty piece of society had worked as a sleeper agent for a Russian mafia splinter group, embarking upon a killing spree which Harry successfully curtailed. Of course, Smith had not been directly investigated for this business oversight. Who could blame him if foreign spies aren't properly vetted before being allowed into the country?

Climmy laughed in awkward embarrassment. He and Smith had never publicly acknowledged this detail, instead choosing to ride on the coat tails of Harry's success.

"It did us no harm, my friend." Climmy countered, the shiny-headed little man smiling with bravado. "The tabloids came close to making a link but it was a coincidence anyway, so we're innocent. The television people loved us. Did you see Stephen and me on daytime TV? We were treated like royalty in the States, all thanks to you taking on that case we handed you, and paid well for too, Amigo!"

"And what's next?" Harry asked, feeling no remorse at touching a nerve. It was satisfying to remind people like these, whose operations weren't for any noble cause, just power and money, that their lives were as fragile as everyone else's.

"Yeah, yeah, of course, mate." Climmy downed some coffee to whet his palate - does this guy need a dosage of caffeine? "This old American bloke dies and the farmhouse takes a couple of years to come on the market, it's been untouched since then, and we buy it based on the recommendations of our representative, he's bloody excited about what's in the barn, all we can see are major development opportunities! Are you with me?"

Again the tease hangs tantalisingly in the air, like Climmy is trying to build a sense of suspense but all he is doing is tightening Harry's impatience.

Stephen tapped Climmy lightly on the arm, which causes a start. Something unspoken passes between the two men. Stephen nodded in a manner which speaks to nobody else but Climmy, who takes seconds to decipher.

"Yeah, yeah." Climmy says, then turns back to Harry. "Your umm- lady friend. She's a property developer agent, right?"

"That's right."

"We were wondering if she might like to take on this job for us? Should be right up her street or, in this case, cul du sac!" Climmy laughed at his win little joke.

"I feel certain she would consider it." Harry acknowledged. "Obviously there's something important in the barn?" Harry prompts. "So, what's the job you want Crane Investigation Services to tackle?"

"I was getting there, my friend. So umm- yeah, we got a bargain to begin with. We were also lucky that nobody else but out our guy looked in the barn. He tells us that it had its own power generator because everything inside was like untouched by the passage of time since the owner's death. It's a miracle, really. It was like an automotive showroom. Makes sense, I suppose, because of the guys background. He had collected antique cars and bikes, some limited editions, or whatever the correct word is. Anyway, he kept records. Never chucked anything out according to our representative. Paperwork going back years. So he found a scrap of paper with details of the stolen James Bond Aston Martin DB5 once driven by Sean Connery in Goldfinger." Climmy pauses to see if Harry is impressed, which he is not, so continues. "This car has been missing a quarter-century and here we are with a potential lead to its whereabouts."

Climmy laughs, looking casually around at the cafe patrons while also making sure that nobody is ear-wigging into their conversation because his tone rose from hushed conspiratorial to excited blasé nonchalance. When he is satisfied that nobody cared what this trio of men had been discussing, he turned back to Harry.

"This could be the find of the millennium." Climmy's eyes were alight with the prospect of the fortune and glory which such an opportunity could offer. "Are you able to go to the farmhouse this afternoon?" Climmy asked perfunctorily. "Our representative will meet you there. Take your lady along too, if she's available, might as well get that ball rolling too. It goes without saying we will pay all your expenses, that's for both of you, plus double your firms usual fee."

Money talks. Business is business. And this offer was obviously not one which the firm of Crane Investigation Services - & Associate - were going to turn down.

# CHAPTER FIVE

When Harry returned to the Crane office he had already contacted Parisa and arranged to collect her at three o'clock that same afternoon. Daphne was busy as usual at the computer in the outer office, tapping away at something, raising her eyes briefly and saying hello before continuing. Zero was sat in his office chair, feet upon the desk, feigning the act of catching forty-winks.

"He's attempting to make a point!" Daphne said without interrupting her typing flow. "Like he's been busy! He could always get us some lunch."

Zero cracked a grin: "I have been busy. All morning! I looked through half of those exciting personnel files from Carlson & Whimpole which you uploaded for me. It's made my eyes tired."

"Now you know how I feel." Daphne retorted. "Fresh air and lunch will help before you restart."

While swinging his legs off the desk, standing and stretching his limbs, Zero said under his breath to Harry: "I hope your case is more interesting."

"Don't worry, dear." Daphne called out. "Your two o'clock will brighten your day. Better put on some of that special aftershave."

"Magnificent." Zero's eyes brightened, and he asked Harry again about his case with Stephen Smith.

"Most probably a wild goose chase. But they're the ones paying, so who am I to judge." Harry replied, then he caught Daphne's attention. "Can you find out all the information there is on…" he was hesitant to say because the whole idea sounded utterly ridiculous "…a 1960's Aston Martin DB5 used in the James Bond film Goldfinger."

Zero's attention and interest was obvious: "The missing one?"

"That's what I was told." Harry said, and explained everything which Climmy had told him about the recluse, the abandoned farmhouse, and car collection in the barn. He finished, saying: "Which all sounds a bit far-fetched to me, but…"

"Far-fetched!" Zero was bug-eyed with shock at his friend and colleagues naivety. He looked at Daphne, who rolled her eyes, knowing where Zero was going. "This is amazing. And Daphne doesn't need to do any research. I mean, I'm a fan. I know the story. Wow." He looked wistfully at a black and white photograph hanging on the wall with his various diplomas, certificates and family pictures. It was an iconic print of Sean Connery casually leaning against the Aston Martin DB5, taken in the Austrian alps. "That's the car." Harry followed his gaze. "BMT 216A." Zero's eyes shone with a hero-worship like reverence. "It was Aston Martin's prototype of the DB5, registration number PPW 612A, and was originally painted red. Special effects expert John Stears made all the gadgets. There were two cars used in the film, and a couple more were used for promotional purposes. This one ended up as a display in an American gimmicky restaurant in the early seventies after being sold by Charlie Chaplin and having its gadgets removed. It was then sold to some rich private car collector in Utah." Zero said this as if it was sacrilegious that such a historically important piece of film memorabilia should be hidden away. "He was having the gadgets retro-refitted by a specialist company when it was stolen, never to be seen again. This was 1997."

Harry nodded silently, absorbing the details.

"So you see," Zero concluded, "it's not only iconic but it's the most famous car in the world. Since mysteriously disappearing dozens of professional detectives and amateur sleuths have scoured all the clues and facts available, and drawn a blank. There has even been a filmed documentary on the hunt for that car. And now..." Zero once more looked dreamily at the photograph, "...and now we have a chance to be a part of the legacy. Amazing."

"We shall see." Harry told him with less optimism in his voice. "I don't know what I'm expecting to find at the farmhouse, might be nothing that leads nowhere."

"All this chatter is fetching lunch." Daphne nagged, tongue-in-cheek.

"Unsubtle hint taken, darling." Zero acknowledged. "What are you having?"

"A bacon and Brie panini, please, dear."

"Tuna baguette for me, cheers." Harry said. "Anything you need me to do?"

Zero turned at the doorway and grinned: "Sure. Let me have the DB5 case." He held up his hand, "no need to answer straight away!"

When Zero was out out of earshot, Harry asked how he was handling the stress of the firm being sued.

"Brave face." Daphne said. "Truth is, I'm pleased he's here in the office doing the paperwork. I can keep an eye on him here."

Harry nodded, accepting her words because she was one of the most wise women he had ever met. Daphne kept track of every case, she was able to get ninety percent of their clients at face value, and she thought the world of her husband and Harry. Her stability was what kept this firm running as smoothly as it did through the ups and downs and the unpredictable, sometimes long, hours.

# CHAPTER SIX

Leaving the coastal A140 road at the second roundabout in Roughton from the Norwich direction, Harry headed eastward on the B1436 Felbrigg link road. The cars sat-nav helpfully instructed him to take the first left after seven-hundred yards, which is exactly what he did. After he did so, the sat-nav repeatedly nagged him that he had reached his destination, was now off-road and to make a U-Turn.

"Shut up." Parisa said as she silenced the disembodied voice.

"Can't be far." Harry commented.

"Let's hope not."

The lane down which they travelled was barely wide enough for the car without clipping its wing mirrors on the overgrown hedgerow, vicariously dotted with no-entry and private signage. Twisted branches of oak trees created an overhanging canopy, causing the cars headlights to activate automatically. Dark vines wound uncontrolled up and along and around the trees and hedgerows on both sides. It was a dark and oppressive tunnel which burst into light after exiting at a brand new sturdy steel gate, likely erected prior to the sale of the property. Beyond, in a circular trodden down area, was a car and Smith's representative.

Harry trundled into the turning circle and stopped alongside the reps car, which was a twin-exhaust Ford Mustang in red on a new plate. The guy was on his phone, which he promptly disconnected, and walked toward them as they stepped out of their car.

"Good afternoon." The rep extended his hand. "You must be Harry and Parisa." He shook a hand in turn, his bright blue eyes full of youth and enthusiasm, while he told them his name is Gary. "Ready to take the tour?"

"Lead on." Parisa said.

He did just that and they followed, Parisa slipped her hand into Harry's. The afternoon sun shone brightly over the tree-lined corridor which had been the darkened lane behind them, skimming the chimney-topped farmhouse which dated back to the late nineteen thirties. The dull red clay roof tiles were smeared with green fungi and ancient bird dropping, and the twin chimneys, despite being a splendiferous feature, sagged where the dry mixture between the bricks had crumbled.

"You're a property agent?" Gary asked Parisa, the enthusiasm bubbling in his voice, pitched quite high and fast as if afraid that time was fleeting.

"That's right. And this is right up my street. I can see amazing potential in this." Parisa said.

"You don't want to just raze it to the ground?" Gary asked. He preferred to start from scratch, build anew, and couldn't yet see any fascination with developing an existing building: "out with the old, in with new, right?"

"These…old facades, have more character." Parisa told him. "Although it's up to the buyer, of course, but with most people I've worked with their preference too is for renovation, rather than a clean slate. That's why people buy up these old properties. If they want something new, they buy a plot of land and build from scratch. I've always ascribed to building on land where a house already exists. I don't like razing nature for the sake of arrogance."

Gary nodded thoughtfully, not entirely convinced because the way of humans is to destroy nature for their own convenience, that's just the way it is. Conservation has its place, of course, but in Gary's mind, he has a paying job to succeed at no matter what a clients preference. He can acknowledge the arrogance of man is ruining the planet but what can he do about it? That's the purview of those in power, the billionaires who can make a difference if they choose to. Not someone like Gary.

The two-storey farmhouse is oblong shaped red brick, six windows front and back, two windows either side, and a front and back door positioned perfectly central. These were the designs of the austere thirties when practicality was more important than aesthetics. Everything is in need of repair or replacement. The windows and doors are white framed UPVC, likely fitted at the turn of the millennium, weather worn and dirty, while what should be clear plastic double-insulated windows are permanently smeared. The red bricks are pitted yet look sturdy, a testament to the construction, but in places the mortar has crumbled and created sags in the walls.

"Can I look inside?" Parisa asked.

"Sure." Gary said. "Its a bit damp and musty, though, despite the long hot summer we have had. And the electricity is off."

Parisa nodded, and let Gary unlock the front door that creaked in protest on its hinges, another sign of age and lack of use. They walked from empty room to empty room which, like Gary said, had a musty smell to them and was uninteresting in their present condition.

"Did Smith have the furniture removed?" Parisa asked when they were back outside, breathing the welcome fresh air once more.

"That's right." Gary said. "First thing he did."

Across the yard, in front of them, the barn loomed large. A taller and longer structure than the farmhouse itself, the lower level was a brick wall with wooden panels sat atop it, while the pitched roof was a combination of wooden slats and Perspex. The concrete apron of the yard led around to the front of the barn, which was out of their line of sight, but it contained the full-height double doors which permitted entry by heavy plant. The barn appeared to be a better maintained structure than the farmhouse, despite vine's creeping up its visible side, where a heavy sturdy, steel door, was bolted and locked.

No machinery was visible.

"Over there," Gary pointed toward the bank of trees which lay beyond the fields, "that's the Ouxerbuey Estate. It's a privately owned castle which is open to the public. The grounds are popular with ramblers. There's a summer fete going on right now. Hard to believe, because there's no noise, and apparently nobody ventures this side of the woodland, either."

The woodland covered a big chunk of land, it's borders weren't visible from where they stood. A spire could be seen, barely perceptible, above the treetops. And, like Gary had stated, there was no noise pollution whatsoever from the fete.

A pair of beautiful Red Kites soured from east to west, circling the border and edge of the fields as the predatory birds majestically went in search of a meal.

"Ready to take a look at the piece de resistance?" Gary asked, a grin of anticipation spreading across his face, knowing what exactly was inside and how stunning a collection it contained.

"Sure." Harry said.

Pausing briefly for effect, Gary unlocked the serious new padlock which secured the door to the wall.

"This isn't the only security measure." Gary told them, knowing Harry would appreciate the fact that a padlock was only as secure as a thief's tools of the trade! When he swung open the door on its well oiled hinges,

Gary stepped through. An alarm beeped its countdown before activation. Gary keyed in a code, killing the alarm. "A sophisticated piece of equipment installed by the owner."

Letting them pass him, Gary watched their reactions as they stepped over the threshold onto the poured concrete floor which, was as smooth as a roller skating rink. Several gleaming automobiles were visible, while some had tarpaulins over them. Harry wondered if Smith, Climmy had  Gary had left their favourites exposed. He imagined their excitement was punctuated when they saw their newly acquired collection. Upon the walls, aligned with each vehicle, were framed posters with highly detailed specifications and historical information, plus other ephemera on the particular models. This was useful for someone like Harry who was a relative novice when it came to classic cars and the like, although even he could identify a Rolls Royce Silver Shadow 1 and a Ford Mustang, but as to their significance, he had no clue.

Harry had immediately noticed that natural light shone upon them from above, while a fine steel mesh running the entirety of the ceiling high above protected the collect from falling debris. A few of the slats had worked loose over time, and some of the Perspex was slightly raised, which permitted bird entry. They could not get further than the mesh though, to which a smattering of feathers and droppings attested.

The deceased owner had clearly loved and cared for his collection, and Harry had to admit that this showroom quality interior was a splendiferous endeavour which he felt privileged to view. One could only speculate from the owners background that it was he who had been proficient enough to tool and equip all this himself, and he had permitted nobody else to view it during his lifetime. If there were memoirs left by the man they would be a fascinating document of the motivation and process behind it all. A motor museum would be proud of such an achievement.

"Impressive." Parisa commented, to which Harry added his agreement.

Gary walked up to a small, squat, white hardtop sports car: "This is a ninety seventy-two Triumph Stag with Rostyle wheel trims, and it's original 2.0-litre six cylinder engine. It's worth today is a fifteen-thousand. This is the lowest resale vehicle here."

Next in line, Gary pointed to what was clearly an older model vehicle, this one a red coupe.

"That's a Jag." Parisa commented.

"That right." Gary said without condescension. "It's a 1954 Jaguar XK140 SE. Currently, in pristine condition, such as this one, they sell for anywhere between one-hundred and three-hundred grand. All the other cars in this collection are around that value or higher. The bikes are worth a bit less, but nonetheless, they're classics by anyone's estimation."

Harry's eyes swept the floor display, counting the total number of vehicles and estimating a top price for the lot somewhere in the region of ten million. Not a bad sum of money for a property which Smith bought at a bargain price. He wondered if the auctioneers of the lot were aware of the massive loss they had incurred by their undervaluation.

"They're lovely cars." Parisa commented. "I have a couple of people I've worked for who would definitely be interested in some of these."

Parisa walked up to a Ferrari F355 GTS which she looked at admiringly, reading the lovingly hung information poster behind it.

Money was often no object to collectors who desired such trinkets, Harry was well aware of that fact, but he couldn't see the fascination which lay in what were ostensibly just pieces of metal, plastic and carbon. He had never had any attachment to the cars he had owned, currently owned, or would ever own. They were tools to get from point A to point B and, with any luck, back again. Nothing more. Unless in the wrong hands, and they could be intentional or unintentional instruments of death and destruction, many examples of which he had witnessed.

"Smith's friend Climmy mentioned something about an Aston Martin?" Harry said.

Gary's eyes lit up more brightly, if that were at all possible. This man was a car fan, or petrol-head, which Harry had already surmised by the car he drove.

Following the younger man to a corner space which had been set up as a duo workspace and office area, Gary sat behind an old, solid work bench, behind which were filing cabinets. It was organised chaos where only the instigator could locate anything straight away. Gary had rummaged here before, because he immediately found what he was looking for: a piece of white card, roughly A6-size, blank on one side, scrawled writing on the other.

Harry took it and read the words: David Brown Five Via Adam Richardson Chassis DB5/2010/R. It was meaningless to Harry. He passed it to Parisa.

"David Brown." Parisa said with instant recognition. "He founded Aston Martin, I think. He's the DB. Adam Richardson…I have no idea. But the chassis number-"

"Is the missing DB5." Gary finished for her. "But before you ask we have no idea who that other guy Adam is either. Which I figured is why Mister Smith has gotten you involved."

Harry turned the card in his hand. He knew that Daphne Crane could simply search the name Adam Richardson on the internet, but would undoubtedly come up with millions of options. Linking it with Aston Martin or Car Collectors as part of the search might narrow it down. Harry sighed: this is what they were paid to do. It's Smith's money wasted.

"A couple I've worked with in Dereham might be able to help." Parisa offered, revelling in the excitement of this potential discovery. She pulled out her phone.

"I was going to set Daphne on the trail." Harry told her. "But I guess it's worth a try."

"Great. I'll set up a meeting."

## CHAPTER SEVEN

Harry drove in the reverse direction along the A140, before cutting through the Norwich City outskirts onto the A47 and heading toward Dereham. Parisa had got through on the phone straight away to her car collector friends, Bernie and Jane, who fortuitously were at home that particular evening. Parisa explained to Harry that she had helped with their house purchase two years ago and seen to the development and upgrade, along with setting up the garage which facilitated their collection. Apparently the pair owned several public houses in the region. Both were devout motorsport enthusiasts, with a collection of mostly modern cars and they would definitely have connections to that world of collecting. This would be right up their alley, and maybe even interested in acquiring the Ferrari F355 GTS which Parisa herself had admired.

When they reached the private cul-de-sac with its pole mounted cameras and Private: No Turning signage, the house they sought was second on the left. An eight-feet tall wrought iron gate situated in the equally imposing wall, parted for them twenty-seconds after their arrival, Harry drove through onto the smooth concrete forecourt.

Bernie and Jane appeared from the house as the gates swung shut. Harry cut the engine.

The couple were similarly dressed in designer vest tops, shorts and crocs, and were in their early thirties, although in Harry's mind she was the younger of the two. Both were of average build which they kept in shape with physical exercise. He had black hair, cut short and tight at the neck, while her hair was blond and styled as if she had just returned from the salon.

Their home was a modern, angular three-storey affair made from steel, breeze-blocks and glass. It was a modest size, suiting their needs without being showy, and sided by trees didn't look too incongruous. The garage was cream coloured corrugated alloy, much like one would find in the pit lane at a motorsport venue. Elongated, squat, and decorated on the outside with badge motifs from a variety of automobiles.

During the exchange of greetings and salutations, Harry took an instant liking to this exuberant and friendly couple, who made a person feel immediately at ease and loose with conversation. They were the kind of rich business people who were without show or bluster. Down to earth and humbled by their good fortune was how Parisa had described them on the car journey, and Harry was now in complete agreement with that assessment.

While Bernie and Parisa talked properties and locations, Jane took Harry by the hand and led him into the garage. The cars inside did not appear phenomenally expensive, certainly not a supercar level of performance, but they were undoubtedly beyond the price range of the average person, and all shone and gleamed like treasured heirlooms. As Jane showed him a car at a time Harry was drawn in by her enthusiasm, gaining some appreciation for the machines on display, but mostly because they each had a history to either herself or Bernie, or both of them.

Eventually, Parisa and Bernie joined them.

"What do you think, Harry?" Bernie asked.

"I had that one myself." Harry said with a smile, pointing to a blue Ford. "In the late nineties."

"Harry's not a petrol head." Parisa said.

"We're all different." Bernie said, matter-of-fact. "That one is my favourite." He pointed to a white Lancia, and gave Jane a knowing smile. "Lots of memories there. Jane and I met when I was was doing a few circuits at Snetterton in it."

"It was love at first sight." Jane explained. "Me and the car!"

They all joined in the laughter.

"You guys haven't eaten, have you?" Bernie asked out of hand.

"Not yet." Parisa responded, Harry shook his head.

"Excellent." Jane said. "Let's go inside then, because I've really worked up an appetite this afternoon," with a hint of subtext, "and I could also do with a drink."

"Sounds like a plan." Bernie agreed.

Harry and Parisa didn't bother to argue or claim that they didn't want to be any trouble, what was the point? Parisa had already told Harry on their journey that they would undoubtedly be invited for dinner. The kitchen diner cover the length and half the width of the first-floor, facing the rear garden which was set to lawn sided with tall pine trees. The layout was all modern angles with no curves, and of grey and white cupboards and surfaces. The central dining table had stools, not chairs, and could seat ten people without feeling crowded. Naturally lit from outside, a few spotlights in the ceiling and table would come on when it was too dark, presumably powered by the solar panelling on the angular rear roof.

"Parisa said you're a private investigator?" Bernie said with no hint of the condescension that usually comes with such a question.

"That's right." Harry said.

"It must be really exciting." Jane probed, while setting out large plates for them all, and bowls of salad, quinoa, and vegetarian delights.

"It certainly has its moments." Harry agreed. "But to be honest it's mostly cheating partners, missing dogs and sitting around waiting for something, anything, to happen!"

"Can you remember the bomb in Berlin from last year?" Parisa asked. "That was Harry."

"Impressive." Jane said.

Bernie pulled the cork from a bottle of wine, sounding a very satisfying plop. He poured the golden liquid into the four glasses on the table.

"So what's this you've come to see us about?" Bernie asked inquisitively.

While they ate what turned out to be a delicious dinner, with a selection of homemade salad dressings, Harry told them about the farmhouse and the contents of the barn, with Parisa filling in a few details about the cars themselves.

"Will this guy Smith sell it all?" Jane asked.

"I'm sure he will." Harry said. "The man isn't exactly a sentimentalist. He's solely out for money and the acclaim which a find like this can bring him."

"Oh, he's one of those type."

"Very much so."

Bernie asked: "What's the detective connection?"

Harry gave a brief explanation of the previous case which Crane Investigation Services provided for Smith, adding a humorous description of Climmy, with a potted opinion of the two Londoners and the aftermath from the successful completion of their assignment.

"They want Harry," Parisa said, her eyes glinting, excitement unhidden, "to find out if this dead recluse was connected to the stolen James Bond Aston Martin."

The room fell momentarily silent. It was a stunned silence while the couple absorbed this information. Harry could understand why. It still seemed absurdly far fetched to him. And yet, if anyone had told him beforehand what he would find beneath the very streets of Berlin last year, he would have questioned their sanity. He smiled inwardly. His friend Michel Lome would point out Harry's cynical nature will always be proved unfounded in reality, or some other convoluted explanation while Michel looked up the facts in his extensive library. Maybe Harry would contact his friend about this. It wasn't necessarily up his street, but his assistance could be invaluable.

"That would be amazing." Jane finally said with a wistful sigh, sipping the wine dreamily.

"What err- lead, have you got?" Bernie asked.

Harry had written down the details from the card which Gary had shown them in the barn. He handed Jane the piece of paper with his neatly copied writing upon it. She passed it to Bernie after casting her eyes over it.

"David Brown is obvious." Bernie said. "And I guess the chassis number matches the missing car? Adam Richardson, though. That's not a name I'm familiar with."

"What about JP." Jane suggested.

Bernie nodded thoughtfully. "Sure. If anybody would know, it would be JP."

"Who is JP?" Harry asked.

## CHAPTER EIGHT

"We pay our solicitor enough!" Zero gesticulated angrily in Daphne's direction while he paced the small outer office carpet of Crane & Associates Investigation Services. His wife watched, perplexed by the rant, much used to her husband's occasional tirades at external office politics. In this particular instance, she could understand what irked her husband. "So why can't he earn his money? What's so difficult with keeping us informed? Communication is key! And it's just a piece of paperwork, that's all! He should see that these loonies who think they have a claim against us go away. How difficult is that, really? We know we did nothing wrong. We acted in good faith by taking them on as a client anyway! It's just because they see that we are successful, and nobody in this country likes success, right! We're not rolling in money. Certainly not the sum they're asking for! Fleecing us! That's it!"

Harry opened the sound-proofed office door. The door was clear glass, so Harry saw Zero's pacing and anger, and knew that it was not good.

Zero stopped talking, stopped pacing, and stopped emoting.

"Good morning." Harry said in a suitably exaggerated voice, closing the door behind himself.

"And another thing," Zero said to Daphne, "that woman yesterday afternoon, she was a delight. Her partner is cheating on her be she is cheating on him! She referred to her partner, the one she wants us to check on, as her lover! What was that all about? She didn't need a detective, that's for sure. Anybody who looked the way she did," to Harry, "she was a bombshell, " to Daphne, "and referred to a partner as a lover is not unfamiliar with cheating or being cheated on! I'm sorry, maybe I'm being a little insensitive but she fit a stereotype. Strewth, we do get them!"

The office went briefly quiet. Zero exhales the remainder of his stress away.

Harry went to the coffee machine which grinds into action.

"Better now, dear?" Daphne asked. "Good morning, Harry."

"Good morning. A lovely one it is, too."

They all laughed, any tension broken.

"That feels better." Zero said, wiping his eyes free of laughing tears.

"There's nothing like healthy expression of emotion to begin the day." Harry said, handing Zero a coffee before making a second one for himself. Daphne already had a steaming mug full within reach. "Daphne, would you mind arranging a meeting for me with Stephen Smith for this morning, please?"

Daphne nodded.

"How is your light and fluffy case?" Zero asked.

Zero and Harry sat in the larger of their two offices while Harry ran through the events and discoveries from yesterday, plus the potential lead which Parisa's friends put him onto.

"So you're going to France, then?" Zero said with faux irritability.

"Probably. Sorry. As long as Smith will pay, which I'm sure will be no problem, he is, after all, seeking a bit more fame. Anyway, how is your case with the research and development firm going?"

Zero rolled his eyes.

"Don't complain!" Daphne said from the outer office, sensing her husbands response. "They're paying us very well."

"Yes, they are," Zero agreed then, to Harry in a hushed voice, "but that doesn't make it anymore interesting, though."

"Stop complaining!"

"No, dear." Zero told Harry: "I'm actually going to their facility today, which is a bit of a rarity, from the sounds of it. They don't admit too many outsiders owing to the work they do there. But they think it might be beneficial for face-to-face, eye-to-eye meetings with some of their people. For some reason they think a detective might gain more insight to a persons character on sight. Who knows!"

"Sounds to me like they don't trust one or more of their employees." Harry said.

Thirty minutes later Harry Kovac was sat in his same seat at the same booth in the same coffee shop as the day before, with the same two people: Stephen Smith and Climmy. To Harry, the time since taking on their latest job hadn't seemed just twenty-four hours ago, maybe it was the company! After they ordered coffees and pastries, black Americano and a cinnamon swirl for Harry, he filled them in on his discoveries from yesterday. They were a rapt audience, Climmy excitedly fidgety, Smith a zombie.

"Bernie and Joan's, JP," Harry finished, "lives in the Dordogne region of France, and apparently he is our next best option, but it would mean me going there for a day or two to find out if she can possibly help."

"No worries, my friend." Climmy told him.

"I can't promise anything, though."

"We know, buddy, but it's all good. Either way we're onto a winner. We got a bargain. Not just the land, but the cars. We've been in touch with your lady, Miss Dane, and she's happy to partner with us when selling it."

"That's good."

"Why don't you take her with you, my friend? To France. If she's not got no other jobs on of course."

"Well-"

"We'll pay all expenses. Don't worry, buddy, either way we win."

"But we will need a place to stay and it's the tourist season."

"No worries, my friend. Stephen and I were out there a fortnight ago with friends of ours. A couple of actors. Jacques and Gillian. We've known them for years, since our time in Vegas with Vic Fontaine, the singer. Those were great times, I can tell you. Did I tell you about them!"

"Yes." Harry replied, pretending interest while hoping to placate Climmy so he didn't have to listen to anymore name dropping.

"Oh, well, good, anyway, Jacques and Gillian have a villa there which they sometimes rent out. I can have a word. See if it's available for a few days."

Harry swiftly downed the remainder of his coffee and rose from the seat. "I don't want to seem ungrateful, but if I'm going to be away from the office for a few days, there are a few things I need to tie up first."

"Sure, my friend. We'll contact your secretary when the arrangements have been made."

"Okay. Thank you." He nodded to the emotionless Smith, and avoided a handshake from Climmy.

"All fun and games!" Climmy said jovially.

# CHAPTER NINE

The caretaker of Villa de'Remy in Vitrac, just outside Sarlat-la-Canéda, waved at Harry Kovac and Parisa Dane as he drove away from the property. The Frenchman had been friendly but stoic, informative and helpful with local details that might be useful during their stay. And he left them a jar of pate which his wife had made, plus a bottle of strong fifteen-percent alcohol white wine produced locally.

It was the day after Harry's meeting with Climmy and Stephen and, despite Harry's feelings towards both those fellows, he had to admit they had certainly pulled a few strings via their connections and come up trumps. They had been able to arrange five days for Harry and Parisa to remain at this well maintained, beautiful villa in a lovely valley within easy reach of amenities and, most significantly, near to where JP lived.

JP had been described to them by Bernie and Joan as an eccentric playwright, artist, and Bohemian woman in her forties who very rarely left her estate in France. She was single through choice, preferring the company of cats and the pleasure of automobiles. JP had a one-and-a-half mile racetrack encircling the internal perimeter of her property, which Bernie and Joan had used on their frequent visits. JP's car collection was, in their words, second to none.

Parisa had JP's number programmed into her smartphone, and a meeting with her at somewhere called Domme, had been arranged for the next day.

What would transpire during their meeting with JP was anyone's guess. She might not have a clue as to the identity of the mystery man Adam Richardson, but with Villa d'Remy as their base and the promise of a few nice days in France with a bit of work included, Harry was determined to make the most of his time here with Parisa, all expenses paid, of course.

First thing Parisa had done once their caretaker guide had gone was to deposit her clothing in the lounge and take a dip in their swimming pool. Harry had joined her, swimming a few lengths, before resting afloat at the deep end.

"It's a hard life." Parisa said from beside him.

"All work and no play."

"I could get used to it."

"Definitely."

They had a basic compact rental car sporting a few de-rigour dents and scratches as mementos from previous drivers, plus over one-hundred thousand kilometres on the clock, but it served their purpose as Parisa negotiated the winding twists and turns on the road from Vitrac to Sarlat-la-Canéda.

They parked in a public area adjoining the usual business park found on the outskirts of most modern towns, it's franchise outlets and restaurants drawing in the average shopper with their bright slogans and promises of the best prices for miles around.

There was a light breeze stirring the hot early evening air which made their walk to the main High Street, Rue de la Republique, more pleasant than it would otherwise have been. The traditional shops and cafes were in a pedestrian zone, so it was nice to walk freely without worrying about traffic. Like most High Streets, this one had various alleyways leading to other shops and exclusive boutiques, offering something for all tastes and price ranges.

Neither Harry nor Parisa had been here before so they enjoyed rambling at a slow pace, much like all the other tourists. Harry wasn't much for shops or shopping but enjoyed Parisa's company, her hand in his, and although more a people observer rather than a people watcher, Harry could not help but notice the majority of expressions were a mixture of miserable, downtrodden, or a zombie-like melancholy. He wondered why a person would choose to not enjoy their holiday. Why could people not be appreciative of how lucky they are?

Harry stopped. He turned to face Parisa, taking her by surprise, and kissed her full on the lips in an uncharacteristic display of public affection.

When they parted Parisa was flushed, panting and speechless.

"Thank you." Harry said to her, and they walked onward.

"What, err- for!" She asked tentatively,

"Being in my life."

Harry proudly walked beside her. Parisa gave him a sideways glance, smiling, eyes moistening with tears of joy. He hoped their pleasure would somehow transfer to those around them. Now Harry thought about it, there weren't really too many miserable faces. He had exaggerated a higher percentage based solely on his own happiness, he was biased because his frame of reference for the day was heightened by his mood. He knew that. Harry was blessed, he knew that, too, and a fortunate man indeed.

People milled around, walked in and out the variety of boutiques, stood in groups, or couples, outside cafes deciding on the one for them, while many others were sitting or standing, eating or drinking or both. A very broad cross section of humans going about their evening after their own unique daily experiences.

Parisa stopped at the window of a local estate agents, located next door to a phone shop selling unnecessarily expensive and elaborate cases and covers, and studied a few of the properties for sale. While following Parisa's gaze when she pointed out something of interest, Harry's sixth sense was triggered by a woman reflected in the window from afar. She had a metaphorical aura about her, a vibe which it seemed only Harry could detect. What that aura was had an undefinable sense of self and surroundings, like a professional who was trained at observing, like an officer of the law or other agency, or perhaps something less scrupulous. Or maybe not. That was why her aura was undefinable.

In the split-second it took Harry to turn around, the woman had melted into the crowd of people at an ice-cream parlour.

Might be nothing, he thought.

"Let's find somewhere for dinner." Harry said. "I don't know about you, but I've certainly worked up an appetite this afternoon."

"I don't know what you mean."

They walked and stopped at a few cafe frontage points to regard the menu until eventually one appealed to them both: Le Petit Maisonette. An unoriginal name but it was not a chain or franchise- in England it might be called The Dunes if it was by the beach - so there were no fake refined frills, no printed menu. The board was handwritten in elegant script, maybe different every day, perhaps done by an artistic family member or employee. Either way, it appealed to both Harry and Parisa's sensibilities.

A waiter bedecked in a tuxedo read their minds and approached them, offering a warm, sincere smile.

"Bonjour monsieur, madam. A table for two?"

Was it so obvious they were English?

"That would be lovely, thank you."

The waiter led them to an outdoor wicker table with cushioned wicker chairs, a glass top with a single stem red rose in a small vase, two washable polyester placemats and coasters atop. The waiter held the chairs for them, politely hovering while they sat.

"May we get a bottle of champagne, please?" Harry asked.

Parisa raised a quizzical eyebrow.

"Certainly, monsieur. Any preference?"

"A Moët, if you have one in your cellar."

"But of course." The waiter nodded approvingly. "Our menu is on the board there, monsieur, madam."

"Thank you."

"Thank you." Parisa said and, once the waiter was tending their drink order: "Champagne? What are we celebrating?"

"We are celebrating how fortunate a man I am."

Parisa regarded him lovingly, her eyes wet but willing away the tears of utter joy which she felt being in his company and extolled so much by Harry. They might not be in Paris but the romance of this French province had gotten the better of her, too. She was very much in love with Harry and was already plotting in her mind to show him how much when they returned to their villa.

The waiter soon arrived and uncorked the wine bottle, dripping with moisture from its removal from the chiller. He poured them a flute each. After taking their food order, the waiter left them once again.

Parisa picked up her beverage first and they toasted.

"I'm the lucky one." She said, glancing in an unintentionally seductive manner over the rim of the champagne flute.

Harry drew his to his lips but paused. Someone caught his eyes. It was the woman again. It was a certainty she had followed them and was now observing from a position outside a cafe practically opposite theirs. She was trying her best to act indiscreet, drinking a coffee, probably decaf. But she was definitely watching Harry and Parisa. A professional. New to the trade. Not a threat. So working for a law enforcer.

"Excuse me a moment." Harry said to Parisa.

Without taking his eyes off the woman, Harry rose from the chair and covered one-hundred yards in barely a heartbeat, but not in a way to attract attention. The movement was carried out at the moment a couple walked between the woman and Harry, momentarily obscuring her view, and while she had a waiter asking her a question.

When Harry arrived at the table, the waiter was walking away.

"Good evening." Harry said to the woman who was startled for a second, then her eyes showed the defeat behind them. "Interpol?"

"That's right, Mister Kovac." She was French. "Is it that obvious?"

"I apologise for ruining your evening, but I'm sure you don't want to ruin mine. Care to explain why you are following myself and the lady?"

"Parisa Dane." She said confidently. "We know you both, Mister Kovac."

"But I'm the one you are watching."

"That's right. Since your thing in Berlin last year Interpol have been instructed to keep- tabs on you."

"In case I'm trouble?"

"To- facilitate aid should you require any."

'Fair enough. Well, you have nothing to concern yourself with, I can assure, but thank you for your company."

Harry walked back to Parisa slowly, smiling all the way. Interpol were not very indiscreet when it came to putting a stakeout on someone these days, he thought.

"Are you okay?" Parisa asked when she rejoined him.

"Oh yes. It's just the local Interpol agent making sure we don't succumb to any harm." Harry raised his glass. "Cheers."

# CHAPTER TEN

Domme is a fortified medieval town, or bastide, in south western France. Sitting two-hundred and fifty metres above sea level atop a rocky outcrop overlooking the Dordogne river and Perigord, it is a member of The Most Beautiful Villages In France. Less than four miles from their base in Vitrac, Harry and Parisa chose to walk the distance through the beautiful, undulating countryside. The weather forecast for the day was good which made their early morning walk for their breakfast meeting with JP a pleasant one.

They entered the medieval town through its original arched portcullis bereft of a gate for over a hundred years, and the short walk felt like twice the distance to their calf muscles. But it was worth it. JP had most definitely chosen a wonderfully inspirational location for breakfast.

They ambled along the inclining Place de la Halle. Traders were beginning to set out their wares under awnings from the old buildings that lent a somewhat romantic old style ambiance to the entire setting. These were the only hints at commercialism. It was still too early for most tourists so the shops which were open were local traders. There was certainly an almost medieval quality to this location, even in the twenty-first century, with its cobbled streets and narrow alleys amongst the low roofs of the old buildings.

"I think we've stepped back in time." Parisa observed. "It's almost unreal."

Harry agreed.

The restaurant where they were to meet JP sat atop the peak of the rock and overlooked a spectacular vista of tree covered rolling hills, snaking roads and the river with barely a building in sight, and what were visible consisted of castles, churches and other older structures that created a historic picturesque backdrop. A hilltop mast was visible some fifteen miles distant. The restaurant itself was a square brick and cobbled building with slate roof, a modern glass awning and iron tables and chairs wrought locally. A glass and steel screen, waist height, protected visitors from falling off the edge of the rock, running east to west along the promenade. It was a perfect blend of the old and new.

There was no mistaking which of the half-dozen diners was JP. She had vibrant dyed red hair that tumbled haphazardly to shoulder length, framing a face full of urgency and alertness. The yellow dress with a red flower pattern she wore was of a practically transparent material, and it was evident she avoided underwear. She wore white running shoes, and dropped on the floor beside her was a wide brimmed hat and an oversized brightly coloured cloth shoulder bag.

When JP saw them walking toward her at a distance she waved gaily and stood up.

"Bonjour!" JP's voice was husky and her eyes were a powerfully vivid clear blue, penetrating while giving their full attention to whomever they were trained upon. She embraced them both, kissed them on each cheek, and beckoned for them to sit as she retook her own. "Harry Kovac and Parisa Dane." She said thoughtfully, and without any trace of accent. "Evocative names, both of them. Harry is a strong name, very English, but Kovac is Eastern European and you don't have a drop of their blood running through your veins. Parisa is clearly a Persian name, although I'm not sure of its meaning."

"Fairy-like." Parisa said. "It means I have an imaginative spirit."

"Yes, yes." JP nodded then pursed her lips thoughtfully, studying Parisa's features, "Italian and… Scottish, perhaps?"

Parisa laughed gaily: "Irish."

JP clapped her hands delightedly.

Suddenly a waitress appeared at their table. She carried a wide tray which held cups, saucers, spoons, a sugar cube bowl and three cafeterias of black coffee, which she placed in the centre of the table.

"Merci, Mirra." JP said, and the waitress left them. "I hope you don't mind, and I sincerely don't like to be presumptuous when it comes to ordering food and drink for other people, but the coffee here is the best, and we will have an assortment of yogurt, fruit, toast and jams which won't disappoint. If that's okay?"

"That's fine." Parisa said, while Harry nodded in agreement.

A second tray was delivered by the waitress and it was laden with pots of butter, jam, fresh yogurt, assorted fruits and two dozen slices of hot toast.

"Bon appetite." Their waitress bid, and left them to attend other diners.

While they ate what indeed was a splendiferous breakfast, JP gave a potted history of her life from college years through to art school, theatre, painting, fashion, a quick dabble in the music industry, and being a speechwriter for various politicians and celebrities. She loved being single and enjoyed a mixed sexed life, preferring the longtime company of cats and cars to humans.  One day she will turn out her memoirs and enlighten a few of the weary travellers of planet Earth.

"As a Private Investigator," JP noted astutely, "it's natural that you should analyse my every nuance, Harry, and I can see you are good at your job."

"I try my best." Harry replied with a wry smile.

"I'm sure Parisa would concur." JP said with slyness. "How does a person end up a private investigator, if that is indeed the end?"

Harry laughed: "I certainly hope not, but I began as a police cadet, rose up the ranks, lost interest in the establishment and decided to try the private sector in a quieter neighbourhood."

"And how is that working out, Hercule?" JP asked.

"Not as quiet as I anticipated."

JP nodded her understanding. "The quietest are often the worst." She said. "Our friends hold you in high regard." JP said to Parisa. "You've worked with Bernie and Joan for a few years now, they tell my?"

"That's right." Parisa replied. "I first met them when they bought their home in Norfolk and helped to design the rebuild of the old house. They had a landscape architect who designed their garden, and a motorsport technician create their garage to properly handle their cars."

"Which brings us nicely to the business at hand." JP said, her eyes alight with excitement. "Bernie told me about the cars and said something intriguing…about a certain missing Aston Martin?"

"That's right." Parisa said, turning to Harry, who took up the story.

"One of my employers…" Harry said."

"As a private eye?" JP said with a twinkle in her eye.

Harry laughed: "Yes, it sounds ridiculous when you say it like that, but, one of many clients purchased a farmhouse and land and in a barn was a very well maintained collection of automobiles…not just cars, but bikes too. The deceased owner was apparently big in Detroit in his day. Well, in this barn was a scrap of paper which had the name David Brown upon it."

"Cool." JP said. "The DB himself."

"It also had on it," Parisa said, "the chassis number of James Bond's missing Aston Martin."

"For real?" JP exclaimed.

Parisa nodded. JP emitted a low, long whistle, to emphasise her surprise.

"Does the name Adam Richardson mean any to you?" Harry asked.

JP's brow furrowed thoughtfully. She sipped her coffee, her third cup, while Harry poured his third and final. Parisa smiled at him, her eyes big, full, moist. Adolescent thoughts tumbled in his mind. He wondered why and how a beautiful woman could possess him so. Not that he wanted her to stop, far from it. Parisa was the kind of woman who did not play up to the effect she had on men because her ego was unaware of her easy sexuality.

"You know-" JP said after a long moment of thought. "You know, the name is familiar but it's buried in my subconscious somewhere. I need time to mull it over without actually thinking about it too hard. You know what I mean?" She waved away that last question. "Of course you do, it's a condescending thing to say, and I apologise for it but I guess it's a habit, like many flippant phrases." She sighed expressively. "Are you guys here for long?"

"A few more days." Harry replied.

"Brilliant. That gives me all day to churn the name over until it produces cheese. What plans do you have for tomorrow?"

Harry and Parisa swapped a glance.

"Nothing." Parisa said.

"Brilliant. You have now." JP handed Parisa a card from her shoulder bag. Upon it was her address. "Come to my home at eight tomorrow morning. We can have breakfast on the river and, if you will indulge me, I can show you a few of the sights before an afternoon of drunken naked debauchery!"

"Sounds good to me." Parisa said.

"See you guys tomorrow." JP rose from her chair. "I've already paid for breakfast, so stay as long as you like."

"Thank you." Harry said.

And JP was gone in a flamboyant uninhibited flourish of swirling dress and vibrant red hair.

"She was a character." Harry commented.

"I liked her."

"I did too." Harry downed the remains of his coffee. "Shall we walk back now? Before it gets too hot."

"Sounds like a plan to me."

While strolling back along the cobbled commercial high street Parisa insisted on purchasing a ring from the jewellers for Harry. He had only ever worn one ring before, his wedding ring, until the end if his marriage. Reluctantly he let Parisa buy a tasteful silver band which was encircled by faux runic symbols with no meaning to them. It was subtle, unobtrusive and fitted perfectly onto his finger.

"It was obviously made for you." Parisa told him when he slipped it onto his finger.

The return walk to their villa in Vitrac was mostly downhill, which was a blessing for them because the temperature had risen by another ten degrees since their outward trip.

"It must be this hot weather." Parisa declared, with no need for further exposition when they were in the seclusion of their villa grounds and she had undressed, pressing her body against his, lustfully kissing him and helping him out of his clothing.

They made love on the lawn before slipping into the warm water of the swimming pool, where they languished and cavorted until quenched.

Harry got them a bottle of wine from the villa's refrigerator and two glasses, placing them between the two sun loungers, sitting upon one himself and watching Parisa gliding beneath the waters surface.

When she joined him they drank the wine.

"Cheers."

They chatted some before Parisa couldn't help herself, her need for Harry, her desire getting the better of her once more until Harry's phone rang.

He answered.

It was Daphne, telling him the news that Zero had been killed.

## CHAPTER ELEVEN

Harry and Parisa had caught the first available return flight to England which, after a car journey, saw them at Daphne Crane's front door in Sprowston, Norwich, at eight o'clock the following morning. Harry had already had the foresight to contact JP and cancel their day together, giving a brief explanation of why. She was sorry, of course, and understood, telling him that she would have some news for him when he next contacted her.

Parisa embraced the sobbing Daphne on her doorstep, and the pair led Harry indoors. He closed the door behind him gently, not wishing to make too much noise under the circumstances. A radio played softly from the kitchen.

Harry boiled the kettle and made three coffees, taking them into the lounge where Parisa was on a sofa with the tearful and despondent Daphne Crane. He wanted to ask a load of questions but sat in respectful silence, looking into the swirling blackness within his coffee mug, processing his own acceptance of the loss of Zero, his boss and friend. Despite building up a defensive wall in his mind against death over his years in the police force, it was a different matter when it was somebody he knew and respected. He needed all the facts right now.

Eventually, Daphne broke the silence: "Zero was on his way back from Carlson & Whimpole Research when-" She faltered, looked out the window, composed herself, and continued. "The brakes on his car failed."

Harry tensed his jaw. Brake failure! That seemed like an almost impossible thing to happen to a modern car which was well maintained, as was Zero's. But if that's what police forensics had discovered then it must be a fact.

Harry was well aware of their procedures. He knew how thoroughly the car would have been examined. At least it wasn't a fault of Zero's. He had had a lot on his plate, and distractions cause many accidents.

"Nobody else was involved." Daphne said with selfless relief evident in the turn of her voice. "And things were- He was in a great mood that morning!" Her teary eyes were big, lost, confused. "We had heard from our solicitors that the person suing us had dropped the case. Zero was overjoyed. We were planning to celebrate last night with a meal out." Daphne cried into her hands, her body wracked with sobbing spasms.

Parisa put her arm around Daphne's shoulder.

Harry felt helpless. Just as things were taking a positive turn.

Brake failure! First thing Harry knew he was going to do was phone his friend in the CID and find out for sure. Make certain nothing has been missed. But then he shrugged mentally, wondered why he suspected foul play at every turn. Nothing screamed foul play, after all. Zero's task had been relatively simple. The Government research facility wouldn't exactly be a hotbed of devious minds bent on murder! Nothing in the conversations between Harry and Zero had pointed to something insidious transpiring. So why the disquiet in Harry's brain. Why the niggling? Was it just because Zero had been a friend and he didn't want his death to be some meaningless accident?

"It's not fair." Daphne said, wet eyes pleading.

"Life is shit." Harry agreed. "But don't worry about the office or work, I'll sort it."

"What about Teri?"

"Good call. I will contact her. See if she can start early."

"Can you finish the Carlson & Whimpole job?"

"Of course."

"Zero was-" Daphne shook her head as if the notion was daft.

"Zero was what?" Parisa gently prompted.

"Oh, it's nothing."

"Not with Zero"." Harry said. "What was he on to?"

"Nothing. Probably. It's just- Well, Harry, he wanted to review one of the research staff there. That's all. It was probably nothing. But if you could finish that job, it would mean a lot to me. Zero had me find out as much as I could on a man called Ross. He didn't say why. Maybe the company had asked them to. But-" She shrugged and sighed. "I don't know."

"No worries." Harry said. "Are there any other cases he was working on that need prioritising?"

Daphne stared off into the middle distance, lost in thought, mind working through the cases which they are presently engaged upon. There were many to consider and all were important, but none sprang to mind as more so than another.

"I will come to the office with you." Daphne said.

"Not today." Harry told her. "Have the day off."

"I've got a free day." Parisa offered cautiously.

Daphne looked at them both before she smiled and nodded.

"Thank you." Daphne said.

"Marvellous." Harry said. "Well, I will open the office, check the snail mail…"

"You'll need my login to check email." Daphne said, quickly finding a piece of paper and scribbling it down. "How is your case going?" She said as if suddenly recalling where the pair had just come from.

"We have another promising lead." Harry told her. "We should hear from her today. Which reminds me that I should also update Smith."

"That's why you need me…"

Harry held up a hand to quieten her. "Not today, Daphne. We will be fine. Take the day off. Sort out all your stuff first. The business can't do without you but we should be okay for a day or two." Then, to Parisa: "I will see you later."

Parisa arose from the sofa and followed Harry to the front door. They heard a big sigh from Daphne.

"Thank you." Harry said in a whisper.

Parisa kissed him on the mouth then said to him quietly: "I love you, Harry, you fool. Be careful."

Harry arrived at the firm's office half an hour later and the first thing he did, after picking up the few pieces of paper snail mail, was put a phone call through to his CID friend at the Norwich Police Headquarters, DCI Gnanakaran.

Harry!" Came the cheerful response. "What can I do for you?"

Harry explained what had happened to Zero. "If you can find out the facts and let me know, that would be brilliant."

"Of course. Strewth, Harry, that's a blow. Zero was one of the good guys in your business."

"He was that."

"Where do you go from here?"

"We have a new recruit starting. In fact, I'm going to phone her now to see if she can start today. Early. She wasn't due to be with us until next week, but I guess these things happen in our line of work."

"Sure, sure. Anyway, any help you need, you know where to find me."

"Thank you."

"I'll contact you once I have all the facts."

"Cheers."

Harry hung up then immediately phoned Teri Hamilton, who answered after two rings. There was background noise of traffic.

"Hi Terri. Sorry to call you but there's been an office emergency and I was wondering if you are able to start today?"

"Yes. Of course. No problem. I was just heading out to the gym anyway. What's happened?"

"I will tell you when you get here."

"Okay."

"Cheers."

Harry hung up and cradled the phone in the palm of his hand. This was business, Harry told himself. Zero had been a friend. Here Harry was at the Crane offices. Despite all the memories around him, he felt nothing. Was it the trade which was making him emotionless? Was it experience? Was it age? Or was it that just now he had too much else to think about to even contemplate the loss?

Harry dialled out a third time, the call was answered after just a single ring.

"Hello. It's Harry."

"Harry, my friend!" Climmy answered oh-so cheerfully, his voice sounded hollow, like he was in an elevator car or other confined space.

Harry didn't want to know. He told Climmy about France and JP without letting the annoying little man butt in. "But Zero Crane has died…"

"Oh my goodness! I'm sorry." Climmy said, which Harry allowed.

"So I've got a few things to see to before I can get back to your job, but I shall."

"Of course, of course, my friend, no problemo. Take all the time you need. Good grief…I am sorry, buddy."

"Thank you." Harry tried to be sincere but the man was just an irritating person so he hung up.

Harry contemplated the opposite wall. A picture was hung upon it. A peaceful scene of hot-air balloons receding into the distance over mountains. Or were they approaching? The painting was rendered in minimal colours. Pastels, if Harry had to guess. It was a painting which had hung in the office as long as he could remember, only this was the first time Harry had gotten the opportunity to look at it properly, from the perspective of Daphne. Little wonder she chose this calming image.

Unable and unwilling to settle his mind, there was just too much to do right now that couldn't possibly wait, Harry fixed himself a big mug of strong coffee before returning to the chair behind Daphne's desk, accessing her computer and pulling up the file on Carlson & Whimpole Research. The file had multiple sections and subsections with lots of text on each employee which the firm had sent them. Little wonder Zero had been tired out from reading it all. There was much to absorb, and Harry certainly wasn't going to read it all.

Two names had been put into their own subsections, separate from the other hundred and fifteen. Headlined employee 2031138 was a woman called Ekvina Groebber, while employee 2034747 was Winston Ross.

Could either of this pair have anything to do with Zero Crane's death?

Harry looked over both names. He tried conjuring up an imagine of them both before opening their respective files, but he was fully aware that clutching at straws was all he was really doing. Harry needed to be a bit more objective. So Zero had separated these two from the other employees because this was the job the research firm had taken them on for, and now Harry was taking over. At least two names were better than over a hundred to sift through. Zero had saved Harry hours of reading.

The office door opened and Harry expected to see Teri Hamilton when he looked up, but instead there stood a man in his forties dressed in tweeds, even the hat, wearing hunter boots and a walking cane that sported an ornate golden handle of twisting tree limbs. His small beady eyes peered over the pince-nez perched precariously on his greasy nose.

"Good morning." The man said in a plummy voice, rolling the letters about in his mouth like they were a boiled sweet. "Mister Crane?"

"No. I'm Harry Kovac. The associate. How might I help?"

"Ah, Mister Kovac! Better still." He entered the room, closed the door, and poised near the visitor's chair on the opposite side of Daphne's desk. "May I?"

Harry made a simple beckoning gesture with his hand and the man sat.

"What's this about?" Harry asked. "I'm a bit pressed for time right now."

"Aren't we all, my good man. You yourself are currently pressed into tasking the whereabouts of a certain Aston Martin, are you not!"

"What if I am?"

"Clients of mine would like you to cease."

"Good for them."

"They can be quite insistent."

"Who are they and who are you?"

"I'm a representative of theirs."

"Then I have nothing to worry about."

"Not at the moment, Mister Kovac."

"Then that's settled."

"I'm afraid not. You see, I must have assertions that you will cease your search for the Aston Martin."

"That's not my call."

"Then, err-, whose call is it?"

"My clients."

"Then I shall have a word with your clients."

"Best you do."

"Quite."

The tweed man rose stiffly from the chair, picked up his cane, bowed in Harry's direction and departed, much to Harry's bemusement. He shrugged to himself. That had been a swift and bizarre waste of time. Harry doubted Stephen Smith and Climmy would be in favour of stopping their search, no matter what the man said, whoever he was or whoever his client. Warning a person of Harry's nature against pursuing a course of action often has the effect of redoubling the effort, and it was a pity that Harry didn't have numerous distractions on his plate right now, because that's exactly what he would have done. Somebody either didn't want the car found or those who took it investigated, or it's recipient discovered. Why? To Harry, answering that question had now superseded locating the car itself. But it would have to wait.

The door opened once more and this time it was indeed Teri Hamilton.

# CHAPTER TWELVE

Harry Kovac arrived at the tall white entrance gates of the Carlson & Whimpole Research complex situated on the extreme outskirts of Norwich City, just off the Northern Distributor Road. This new land development project had sprung into existence in conjunction with the construction of the NDR upon reclaimed property. Harry had learned from Daphne Crane's thorough research that an old canning factory had once existed here, but after a merger and restructuring the factory was abandoned, which worked favourably for the NDR committee because the land could be turned into a commercial facility once the road was completed. The local council benefited because when the land was purchased it was by a research facility backed by the country's government, which meant a guaranteed income for the land plus accommodation for their employees, and Carlson & Whimpole were themselves relocating from a higher taxation area thus reducing their own costs.

This had been an all-round win-win situation.

This complex exuded newness. Modern surveillance cameras looked down from the clean gateposts. There was no litter blown against or sucked into the heavily bolstered fence, which warned of death by electrocution should someone try breaching it. All that was required was razor-wire topping it's length and this could almost certainly be transformed into a high security prison.

The gates parted smoothly for Harry without him having to get out the car to announce his arrival and credentials, and that could only mean the powers within had his photographic identification and vehicle registration information. Which made sense.

Reinforced steel cylinder blockades lowered into the ground and Harry drove through the gate that soon closed behind him, blockades raising into position. Was their research really this valuable?

Following the tarmac driveway into the car park, which was almost full, Harry parked up, got out the car and a cursory glance concluded there were no security cameras in the car park itself. A curious oversight? Or confidence that their employees would be vigilant and honest? Either way it was an annoyance because Harry had hoped to gain access to CCTV footage for purposes of discovering if Zero Crane's car had indeed been tampered with. And a saboteur would know this. Very convenient for him or her, if such a felon existed. Harry would have to mention this glaring oversight to whom ever was in charge.

Harry strode through the car park towards the white walled and glass fronted two-storey building which was the only conceivable route, warm air unstinting in the natural basin within which the complex sat. Blessed air-con. The car park was enclosed on all sides by a fence, it's only departure point the way which Harry had arrived, and the entrance to the complex. He pushed open the door which hissed when it's seals were parted. Cold air rushed out before Harry was inside and the door hissed shut.

There was barely any noise in the reception area which was like any reception area in a complex of this nature: sparsely furnished, bland, clean, antiseptic in freshness.

"Good morning, Mister Kovac." The voice was from behind the reception desk and belonged to a pristinely dressed woman in her thirties. She wore a crisp white blouse, matching white skirt, flats and her hair was tightly tied back.

"Good morning."

"Sorry to hear about your partner." She offered as she came around the desk. "I have arranged for the ten people you are to interview today to join you in The Restbite at twenty-minute intervals. I hopes that's okay with you?" She asked the final question in a way which told him that it was too bad if he wasn't okay with her plans, because that's the way it was going to be.

"Thank you, that sounds fine." Harry had contacted the firm last night and requested that his two suspects - if one could refer to them as such - could be part of the group he was to see today. There was no mention of this by the receptionist, and Harry didn't press her on the matter.

The receptionist led Harry along an unadorned white corridor, unmarked doors leading to who knew where, until they eventually reached what she had referred to as The Restbite. The room turned out to be furnished with plastic tables, upholstered blue chairs, and a serving area for food and drink.

"Help yourself to drink." She said. "Your first interviewee will be along in ten minutes sharp."

"Thank you."

And she left him alone without a further word.

Harry made himself a strong coffee from the machine and strode through the cool room to the glass double-doors, which opened into a small garden courtyard, surrounded by internal complex walls. It was like a hospital, really, and bore no personal touch. Stoic and all business, much like the greeting he had received. It made Harry smile, thinking about how these types of establishments are almost a parody of each other.

With no more time for introspection, Harry's first interviewee arrived. He turned out to be a senior team member with ten-years experience of Carlson & Whimpole, five of those before the research company changed its name to its present moniker. Harry merely asked the man his opinion on the two people of particular interest, which were bland, predictable answers. It seemed that nobody really socialised after hours. A secretive bunch doing secretive work. Nothing unusual there.

"Whose idea was it to have no security guards or cameras out front in the car park?" Harry asked pointedly.

The man shrugged: "It was designed that way. We aren't an unscrupulous bunch or people, Mister Kovac. At least not here, at work." He laughed weakly. "Nobody gets through the gate who shouldn't get through the gate. If any of us should ding somebody's car…well, I know that we would admit to it straight away, so there's no need for cameras. It would just be something else our two security officers would need to keep an eye on, and there are two on permanent posting here. They already have enough to do, I guess." He shrugged once again. "That's a question for our head office, Mister Kovac. Sorry I cannot be of any further help."

"No matter. Thank you for your time."

The man went on his way, doing whatever his day dictated. Harry wondered if he was being an inconvenience to these scientists while he was here. Not that he cared, really. He was doing his job, they were doing theirs.

The two who followed separately might very well be personality devoid clones. Their answers practically mirrored each other and they effectively confirmed what the first man had said about non-existent out of hours socialising. Harry realised logical scientists were essentially cut from the same cloth, but still, a little variance on the personality spectrum would be refreshing.

Harry stood once more by the doors with a coffee in hand and ponder in mind. Next up was Winston Alfred Ross. Now going by the name Alfie, a futile attempt to separate himself from his father, the ex-politician of dubious renown.

The moment that Alfie Ross entered the room Harry could understand why Zero Crane had taken an instant interest in him. On the surface this guy exuded blandness, but the eyes were shifty, they held a deviousness and agenda which belied the appearance. Alfie wore the standard white smock, trousers and shoes that his colleagues sported. He was approximately five-feet seven, petite of frame, with slightly rounded shoulders through years of leaning over work benches and peering at screens. He had an unkempt mop of silver tinged black hair which looked like a wig but on closer study it was a cut choice. Alfie's features were bland, normal, unspectacular, the kind a mother would love but people wouldn't give a second glance at or remember afterward. But the furtive eyes, ever moving in an evasive manner, which were calculating and bore a definite untrustworthiness that had caught not only Harry's sixth sense, but had undoubtedly been a factor for Zero's interest too.

For the second day in a row Alfie Ross's work routine was being interrupted by a snooping private investigator. He was irritated and slightly concerned - what would his father say now?

Alfie was striding through the central corridor from his workspace ignoring colleagues, which was nothing unusual, while wondering if he had accidentally let something slip yesterday. He was certain he had not. Maybe the detective was better at his job than the hack which Alfie had taken him for. Maybe the stupid, spur-of-the-moment car tampering had been discovered. But, as he tried to remind himself, he was not the only one being interviewed.

Anger broke through. Alfie knew deep down in his psyche that he should not be under suspicion of anything. In fact, the opposite should be the case. He had assisted most profoundly in finding a treatment for the Pandemic which had gripped the globe in 2020. Alfie had spent hour upon hour of time, often forgoing sleep, in the laboratories which had eventually proven fruitful. He, Alfie Ross, had been a hero. Why should he not still be one? What had changed?

Stay safe. Stay indoors.

Those had been the words used during the Pandemic lockdown by those who had enough power to feel infallible. Not necessarily from the virus itself, any human on Earth could have caught it and passed it on, a bit like influenza, but Alfie knew of many, many people who felt infallible to their own rules and had benefited financially from the manmade disruption.

Alfie Ross had aided in putting a stop to the isolation back then, but the corruption continued unabated and it made him and like-minded people furious. Abuse of the system post-pandemic had gone unchecked. And now government and businesses basically wanted to keep control of people with pressure from increased financial demands.

It wasn't a virus killing people now or ruining society this, it was the immense corporate and government corruption, and now enough was enough.

It made him impotently angry.

When Alfie opened the door to let himself into The Restbite he thought at first he had got the wrong room. The person by the French doors wasn't who he was expecting. It wasn't the investigator from yesterday. This was a new guy, and on first glance, Alfie liked him less than the other one.

"Good morning, Mister Ross." The Investigator said, his eyes probing, clearly trying to intimidate, but Alfie was too intellectual to wilt. "My name is Harry Kovac and I represent Crane and Associates Investigation Services.

Alfie Ross smiled at Harry and fetched himself a coffee without saying a word, his expression resigned to the imminent questioning and bored by the prospect, at least that's what he tried to convey. Make the man work for his time, and don't panic.

"Your colleague spoke to me already." Alfie said defensively, his voice a deliberate Middle English without accent, a holdover from his well bred upbringing, now disdainfully applied. "This feels like an invasion of my privacy." He sat at the table nearest to himself, forcing Harry to cross the room in a sign of self-satisfying arrogance.

Harry steepled his fingers, silently studying this man who stirred his coffee with unfettered boredom. Good, Alfie thought, let this man try his worst!

When eventually Alfie looked Harry in the eye he couldn't help but mentally recoil, intimidated by the hard stare which the detective sported and no doubt was pleased to do so. It took all Alfie's resolve to hold the stare, affix his own, trying with difficulty to blank his emotions.

"My colleague," Harry said, "is why I'm here now." He paused, evidently trying to let the worm of doubt weave into Alfie's brain, but he tried not to react, making it difficult to tell. "Yes, my colleague, Zero, thought highly of you. I was hoping to get your opinion on a few things."

What? Really? Alfie's demeanour briefly perked up, his curiosity roused. Bored arrogance changed to suspicious interest. Alfie had picked up on Harry's use of Zero in the past tense but it meant nothing, really. Or did it?

"Oh?" Was Alfie's cautious response.

"He was hoping your extensive experience in this field might offer some insight into the psyche of certain colleagues." Harry said reasonably. "You've worked all your life in laboratories across the country and abroad, so I understand. Zero had been hopeful that you would be able to help him." Alfie's reticence held. "How well do you know Ekvina Groebber?"

Alfie was puzzled. He had never heard the name before until recollection sprung into his eyes.

"Nina." Alfie said, then, thoughtfully. "She's worked here, what, two years now, I guess? But you probably researched that already. Nina's from the Ukraine. She's competent enough. Aloof, I suppose you might call it, but there again we are all a bit aloof here, really. It's part of the intellectual scientific community, I guess. We don't tend to mix socially either, not any of us, that I'm aware of, at least, not even the homegrown ones!"

"My colleague was under the impression that Nina is quite, um, popular with the men?"

Alfie snorted derisively. "That's the first I've heard of it. Unless…" He paused, eking out this line of conversation. "No." He laughed. "Most of us English guys stay clear of anyone who can't be bothered to speak the same language, if you know what I mean."

"What kind of work does she do here?" Harry asked.

"I couldn't say. It's secret. You know how it is."

"Fair enough. How about you, then? What's your field of expertise?"

"Chemical and biological engineering. I have two PHD's. Helped with the virus cure a few years back." Alfie said with great pride and why not, it was no secret. "Little good that did. The Chinese will no doubt develop something better next time. Or the Russians, or Koreans, you name it really, they're all the same. But we can try being one step ahead, I guess. At least that's part of my job here, to save the country."

Alfie sipped his coffee nonchalantly, hoping he hadn't said too much which this detective might find overly offensive, not that he cared too much what people thought of his convictions but it was better safe than sorry in this stupid, maligned world.

"Impressive." Harry smiled ingratiatingly. "What do you think of the new interns?"

"Can't understand a word they say."

"Oh?"

"Yeah, they're all foreigners." Alfie said this disdainfully. "Anyway, is that all?" He checked the clock. "I've important work to do." Which was true, not that this intellectually challenged detective could possibly comprehend what such work entailed.

"Have you spoken to your father recently?"

"What? No. What's that got to do with anything?" Alfie pushed back his chair, the bored expression returning, and drained the dregs of his coffee cup. "I fell out with my father years ago. Surely a detective would know that?"

"Thank you, Mister Ross. You've been very helpful." Harry said. "By the way…my colleague died in a car accident after leaving here yesterday. Would you know anything about it?"

What? Died? Car accident?

Harry had timed this statement and question perfectly it seemed, because despite the cool and collected scientist not missing a beat or hesitating as he ambled across the room, Harry could see a flicker of concern cross the man's face, however briefly it was there. So, Harry thought to himself, Zero had been onto something after all, although Harry was yet to discover what that something was. Winston Alfred Ross definitely had a guilty conscience about something. Could this ineffectual scientist have sabotaged Zero's car, and if so, why?

"I'm sorry." Winston tossed back casually. "I don't know anything about that."

The chemical engineer shrugged indifferently, feigning nonchalance, pretending to fail to see how anything he had said could have been of any use to anyone, even a detective. But Harry was too savvy to be suckered by a guilty man, and this one oozed the metaphorically sublime pheromone which triggered a detectives senses.

Winston deposited his empty cup in the dishwasher and strode out the door without a backward glance, leaving Harry alone with his thoughts.

## CHAPTER THIRTEEN

Harry hadn't been to his home in Wroxton-on-the-Broads for several days and took the extended journey to mull over his visit to Carlson & Whimpole, and primarily Winston Alfred Ross. It didn't take a detective to conclude that Alfie was a no good human being, even if it was solely based on his sexism and racism. But what was he hiding?

Pulling his car into his parking spot Harry's cursory glance at the front of his home included the observation that the lawn needed mowing, a side hedge needed a trim, and leaves required brushing off the path. He sighed. Everyday chores such as running the vacuum cleaner and dusting would also need attention. Thankfully he had used Parisa's washing machine and linen line to launder the clothing from the past few days, so that was one chore pre-emptively solved. Parisa had today travelled up to Scotland for work, where she was to stay overnight.

Harry had already checked his smartphone for messages. Parisa had left him a cheery one, wishing him a productive day, to not forget to check in on Daphne - her parents had come, and she had insisted on tending the office - and Parisa told him that she loved him, before ending the call. Harry had a pair of messages from Daphne. The first was about a job, the second was sent just after noon telling him she was now going home. Daphne had been insistent that she go to work that morning, to which Harry hadn't argued, but wasn't surprised that it was for just part of the day. Zero's widow had much funeral formality to attend to, and the office paperwork was insignificant compared to her upheaval, but Daphne was a strong person determinedly getting on with her life.

As did Harry.

Household chores were just that: chores. A necessary evil if one were to maintain a respectable home. But at least the time spent doing them offered Harry ample opportunity to consider the response and attitude of Winston Ross. Maligned attitude. Clearly the Englishman's Etonian establishment upbringing had imbued him with many old-fashioned, old-boy outlooks on people and life. His opinions on race and culture were what kept him from a pleasant work/social life. As for his secretive nature, that could be explained away by the job responsibilities of a scientist. He was a loner, unmarried, distancing himself from his family, estranged from his influential father. These things would make a person naturally suspicious, cautious, and with an aversion toward personal relationships. The furtive mind, avoidance of eye contact, were also synonymous with such people, especially those who considered themselves intellectually superior. But the poorly hidden reaction upon the news of Zero's death? Maybe he hadn't correctly heard Harry's question. Maybe he hadn't intended to kill? But there had been no remorse. No panic at the news. Just the briefest of tells in Winston's eyes.

So what the hell was going on?

Harry mentally shrugged, wondering if he was clutching at invisible straws. He had no idea what could have motivated the scientist to kill Zero. A suspicious dislike of someone wasn't exactly enough of a motivation. A cold, calculating scientist wouldn't exactly revert to a malicious act on a whim.

So what nagged at Harry's subconscious?

Something else nagging at Harry was his hunger.

Harry's refrigerator and cupboards presented no true inspiration for him. Maybe he didn't really know what he fancied. That was the problem. And what a nice problem to be presented with in a world where poverty in ones own country existed.

The time was now approaching four o'clock. Winston Ross would now be finishing work and have a tail in the form of Teri Hamilton attached. She was indeed a star. There had been no hesitation to Harry's request. He couldn't exactly follow Winston himself without creating suspicion. Teri would let him know the scientist's movements and if anything remotely suspicious happened.

Harry strode out of his home and up the cul du sac, enjoying the fresh air and countryside sounds, occasionally saying a hello or gave a tilt of the head acknowledgment to the few people on his way. Some people were more familiar with him, giving what they believed to be a sly or wry witty comment regarding his job. There was no avoiding it for Harry, really. He had been featured in a local newspaper article pertaining to salubrious events at the TAMS Supermarket in the village, and as he crossed the footpath and weaved through the bike barriers to the side of the store, he couldn't help but recall those events himself. Harry hadn't courted celebrity in his life but it had unavoidably been thrust upon him months ago and, now, people had grown weary of churning out the same remarks, having lost interest, gone on to whatever scandal they now sought to rumour monger.

The cool air conditioning sent a slight chill running across Harry's skin when he entered the brightly lit store, which resembled any supermarket found in England except for a few uniquely local attributes. But mostly it had a generic sight and smell and sound to it.

Harry made a direct beeline for the chiller cabinets, unsure what he fancied but knowing that a ready meal was on the cards. He didn't want to faff around prepping and cooking, not today, not alone.

While browsing Harry felt eyes upon him, sensing an approach before looking up when a TAMS manager was within a few feet. The woman had a pleasant/anxious face, was in her early 30's and wore her uniform comfortably and professionally.

"Hi." Her friendly greeting was genuine enough and without embarrassment. "I'm sorry, but you are Harry Kovac?" She asks unapologetically. "The private detective?"

Harry gave a nod of resignation. "That's correct." He tried not to clench his teeth or tighten his jaw irritably.

"I thought so. Sorry about this." Only she isn't sorry on any level. "We have been experiencing a few…issues with local kids, not from here, not from our village, but from Hoveton. They've been coming here from…well, there's no law to stop them coming here, I guess." She was almost falling over her words in an unmanageable mess. "What I mean is, they've been causing us trouble in the evening. Being rude and intimidating to staff and customers, stealing… Like they don't care, which they probably don't." She concluded with an inevitable sigh of exasperation.

"You've contacted the police, of course?" The question was marked more as a statement because calling the police was the first thing which had been done, and the manager confirmed as much. "Then I don't know how I can help you. It's a bit out of my firms realm of influence."

Now the manager truly was embarrassed. Harry did not have the time nor resources to help the supermarket. It wasn't like he could be there when these children arrived. Yet clearly she was getting desperate otherwise she wouldn't have approached him. What did she expect him do?

"I'm afraid of what might happen." The woman said, her eyes pleading for some direction. Evidently the end of her tether was fast approaching. "They turn up at irregular times, which is why the police are never here. When I phone the police, it's too late, they've gone. I've given them what CCTV footage we possess but still it goes on. It's like nobody cares. I've even tried following these kids to see where they park up because they're clever, they don't use our car park. But they're totally abusive, physically and verbally, and they don't care. Of course, we are told by corporate that our safety is paramount and that we shouldn't put ourselves at risk, but that's easier said than done."

"It sounds as if you are presented with a real problem." Harry agreed. "Your head office won't provide you with a security guard, I presume?"

"I'm sure they will when one of us gets seriously hurt." She says cynically.

"Tell you what I'll do." Harry said. "I'm home tonight." He hands her a business card. "Phone me as soon as they come in. I'm only five minutes away."

There was a visible relief upon the managers face when she took the card from him.

When Harry got home with an English inspired microwaveable meal deal consisting of liver and bacon with mashed potatoes and mixed vegetables, he wondered if he might regret his decision to help TAMS management. After all, it's the retailer's cost-cutting which is preventing investment in a security guard that's the real problem. But never mind, these kids might not turn up tonight. And if they do? He's not so easily intimidated, quite the opposite, in fact.

While his microwave oven nuked what turned out to be a bland dinner - no surprise, really, because he had indeed been spoiled by top quality food for the last few weeks in the company of Parisa - Harry turned on the television in the lounge and sank into the corner seat of his broad sofa, propping his feet up on one of its paired lengths. The news was on. Harry let the newscaster waffle on about some celebrity shenanigans while he checked his smartphone for any messages.

Teri Hamilton had told him in detail of Winston Ross's movements so far since he left work, including times and addresses. Teri was pleasingly thorough and professional with the facts, offering up no theories or idle conjecture.

Parisa had also sent him message, hoping he was enjoying a hearty dinner while telling him that she was staying at a five-star hotel and wished he were with her. He replied with a laughing emoji and a picture of a microwave oven.

It had been an age since Harry had had time on his hands and was at a real loss. There were many things he could be doing right now but his mind reeled with a maelstrom of random thoughts that he became exasperated. Boredom was anathema to him. He knew that one should be careful what one wished for in life, but while he halfheartedly consumed the bland meal, he hoped the TAMS manager would phone him to give him at least something to do before he fell into asleep on his sofa in front of the television, which wasn't a prospect he savoured.

## CHAPTER FOURTEEN

Winston Alfred Ross's body was discovered just after five o'clock in the morning by an exponent of fitness. A woman who rose early, did cardio exercises, went for a run before showering, breakfast and work. It was a routine she tried to adhere to as much as she possibly could, and the early start, earbuds in, meant fewer people. She lived in the same six-storey quadrangle of apartments as Winston Ross, to where he had returned home just after eleven thirty the previous night.

Alfie hadn't realised that he was being followed from work. He hadn't noticed the car which had been parked opposite the Carlson & Whimpole entrance, amongst the other parked cars in the business park. Why should he? The car park was always full of capitalist consumers, the sheep in society who Alfie hated almost as much as foreign interlopers. They took English jobs. They made English society seem lazy because of their initially free-loading exploitation of bureaucracy.

Alfie drove angry to the underground parking facility which the high premium he paid for his apartment could afford. It was a luxury to have such privilege in Norwich, but he had worked hard all his life for his money, so felt a certain entitlement. Maybe such shocking commercial success was anathema to his belief system, especially ironic when he considered the meeting he was attending with a friend later that evening, but at least Alfie had earned it honestly, without exploiting his family position, without exploiting the easily exploited system, and without being a burden to anyone.

And without anyone being a burden to him.

Riverside Retail and Leisure Park was his neighbour, alive even at this relatively early hour in the evening, but not quite so vibrant as when lit up by neon signs. Alfie had nothing against that kind of commercial venture. In his meagre spare time he himself had used what this sprawling complex had to offer, excluding the shops, of course. He enjoyed hypocritically assessing the people who frequented it with his superior analytical skills. These kinds of inner-city facilities drew people together, which was a good thing, in Alfie's minds eye. He was a proponent of such family friendly environments, despite being antisocial himself. But he would often contemplate the financial consequences of people paying exorbitant amounts of money for being there. How could the average family sustain such an expensive lifestyle?

But it was a positive aspect of life, Alfie thought to himself, touching his thumb to the access panel in the recessed lobby of his apartment block.

Government and big business want people to be isolated. They need armchair consumers to stare zombie-like at their screens ordering stuff they don't need, or stream stuff to waste their time from the multitude of devices which zapped their ability to reason. This isolationism has gotten worse in the short few years following the Pandemic, financial pressures forced on the general public by an out of touch government, and the conflicts and disasters which the powers that be blame for inflated budgetary spending.

Alfie knew better than most about the egocentric political power structure built on greed and accumulated wealth. How the rich establishment blamed outside forces instead of looking inward at their own culpability. No, that would mean bucking the trend, changing their privileged outlook, facing up to the reality of life. Instead, politicians and policymakers could see only their world through blinkered eyes, pretending to care about their constituents, acting out empathy when they have none, serving their greater masters: Big Businesses.

Alfie had entered his top floor apartment, stripped, showered, dressed in linen combats and a baggy shirt, and eaten a light dinner of egg noodles, beef strips fried in black bean sauce, and some microwaved vegetables, washed down with a protein enriched smoothie.

Not quite a detox of his body, but tonight's meeting would certainly be a detoxification of the spirit with like minded people. Not with the scientific community. Maybe that would be a more logical way for someone like Alfie to spend his time. To surround himself with intellectual minds and intellectual curiosity. But he would be escorting a female whose mind utterly lacked intellectualism. Alfie found his conversations with females in the scientific community always involved emotion at some point which, in his mind, detracted from any given subject.

Emotions had their appropriate place.

After finishing dinner Alfie returned to the underground parking area and drove his car to a house in the Plumstead suburbs of Norwich. It was an undesirable area where Alfie would rather not be but all he was doing was collecting his friend, so he didn't have to set one foot out the comfortable space which was his car.

Marti Baines was Norfolk through and through. She was forty years of age and had never been out if the county. Marti's philosophy when questioned about her lack of travelling was that she had everything she needed in Norfolk, and had no desire to visit anywhere else. Alfie thought her temperament was meek and perhaps a bit frightened of venturing outside her comfort zone. This naïveté had provided the perfect opportunity for Alfie to exploit her. She could be controlled and manipulated without being aware of what was happening. Better still, she was single and vulnerable. Although Alfie couldn't see any real quality within her that would make her otherwise. Marti had curly brown hair with touches of grey, her pallor was pale, like old cream parchment paper, and physically she possessed nothing which Alfie could see as attractive to man or woman alike.

This nondescript woman got into the passenger seat of Alfie's car, bringing with her a faint damp pet smell. Marti was a cat person. They were the only attachment she had. Alfie was her only friend.

"Alright, love?" Marti asked.

Alfie set his jaw. He hated the Norfolk accent. People sounded slow, backward, like idiots. Most of them were fools, he had discovered. Lugubrious naive fools.

"I'm fine." Alfie replied, stifling a laugh. "How has your day been?" He asked, feigning interest.

"Well, let me tell you-" Marti sighed, exhausted, like she had just completed a triathlon.

Alfie pulled the car away from the curb, pleased with the distraction from this woman who droned on and on about her boring day as a cleaner. He had been accommodating to Marti's nature, patiently listening to the drivel she spouted ceaselessly. Thank God his deception of friendship was finally reaching its conclusion and he didn't have to be civil to this boring cloth-headed colloquial cleaner. A bloody cleaner! The lowest of the low, in Alfie's thoughts. A perfect job for a female, especially so for this particular one.

Fifteen minutes of listening to Marti's prattle later, Alfie pulled his car into a space alongside a new-plate Jaguar in the car park of a village hall in Wroxham. It was a good turn out for The Sanctity of Sunday meeting, like it usually was. Alfie enjoyed the talks, the passion, the almost evangelical nature of the show. And it was a show, to a certain degree, because little could be achieved by these people alone. But the greater group, the wider community, that could affect change eventually.

And after tomorrow?

Alfie smiled warmly at Marti, feeling the excitement through her hand as they crossed the gravel car park to the entrance of the hall. Marti's eyes were wide with surprise. He had never held her hand before. They were just friends, nothing more. To Alfie, Marti was the unsuspecting innocent means to a life-altering end.

After the meeting Alfie dropped Marti at her home and returned to the comfort of his own apartment. He switched on his television to illuminate the lounge, fetched the celebratory bottle of single malt whisky which had been the most expensive the local supermarket sold, along with a tumbler, and sat opposite the fifty-five inch LED screen.

Alfie did not usually imbibe on a week night but tomorrow morning he was going to phone in sick for work. He would claim he had the flu. Nobody wanted to add a biological contagion into a chemical research facility. Excitement and anticipation was getting the better of him. People would notice the abrupt change, and he knew it. Tomorrow was the day that years of preparation and planning had led up to, and he wouldn't be able to contain himself.

He poured a generous measure of whisky into the tumbler and downed it in one go, the heat and alcohol immediately hitting the spot.

Alfie considered getting a savoury snack from the kitchenette to soak up the alcohol so he didn't get drunk too fast, but a second swift snifter made him forget that idea.

A laugh burst forth from him when he recounted the plan to phone in sick tomorrow. The flu! What a genius stroke of irony.

Alfie stabbed the channel changer on his television remote, disgusted at the foreign muck they showed nowadays. Inclusion was ruining this country. Englishmen wanted the country returned to themselves without fear of being deemed imperialist or racist or worse. How difficult was that to achieve?

Finally Alfie found something suitable, a comedy film from the seventies, when humour and beauty were permitted to exist in culture without the sexist feminist brigade casting aspersions. Maybe there would be something for him.

Alfie poured another tumbler half full. He laughed. His life was full, not half full, and definitely not half empty!

Why had nobody stepped up since that stupid woman lasted only a few days at Number Ten, and then a rich foreigner? There was no backbone in politicians these days. Nobody taking a stand on immigration which was proving a ruination to the country.

No more sitting on the fence!

Alfie's plan would commence from tomorrow. It was time for his father to bring the country back from the doldrums, to make it a better place for English citizens.

"Make England great again." Alfie said with drunken pride, his eyes glued to the screen and the bare breasted young female striding unfettered through a farmers field, her naked beau in tow.

Alfie was getting hot. A mixture of alcohol and excitement and the summer night which made him drunkenly undress, dropping his clothes haphazardly wherever they fell around his feet.

The couple on the screen stopped by a tree. He cupped her breasts, then she groped his butt. And what a firm butt he had. And strong legs.

Alfie's pulse raced.

A full-frontal shot of them both.

This was too much for Alfie and he stroked himself into ecstasy.

"Shit."

Alfie hadn't planned for this. Obviously the alcohol was to blame. There were no tissues in easy reach. Stupid! He made a wavering beeline for the bathroom so he could wash his hands and privates before he messed up his furniture, drunkenly losing his balance, but eventually successfully reaching the basin. He laughed. This was typical, and certainly not the first time.

When he was washed and dried he made his way back into the lounge but stopped short. For a split-second he thought his dreams had come true. Two men were standing in his apartment. Big, hard men. The type Alfie liked. But what initially appeared to be his lucky night, soon turned into a nightmare.

## CHAPTER FIFTEEN

Fatal Wealth and Hellbeing were the words Harry thought he had read as the byline atop the flier which Teri Hamilton handed him next morning at the Crane Investigation office, and despite the inaccuracy and slightly inflammatory nature of it, the declaration might still fit with The Sanctity of Sundays mission statement.

What it really read, now that Harry had turned the flier over in his hand to face himself, was Family Health and Wellbeing. This was definitely a more appropriate statement for a group extolling the old-fashioned virtues of Sunday being a day when family and friends should spend time together, instead of attending retail outlets like religious substitutes. They were certainly required in this age where individuals had isolated themselves from the outside world. The aim of The Sanctity of Sunday gathering, it seemed, was to encourage the Government and Church into making a sea change to their policies and force retailers into closing their businesses on Sunday, and thus restoring the day for families and friends to be together without burden of work or shopping.

A noble cause, Harry admitted to himself, but one which was impossible to achieve.

Last nights topic was, apparently, Societal Ennui. Described as a thought-provoking discussion about the importance of social justice and how to address the challenges facing our communities though positivity. Society has apparently been sleepwalking through life without thought to addressing the need to question who, or what, is creating this society, why they are creating it, and debating how to reverse the ennui.

"Lofty goals." Harry commented after reading the flier. "And good propaganda."

"Good luck to them." Daphne Crane offered from behind her desk. "I have some news." She said, tapping away at the computer screen before her. Her face dropped. "It's never ending, is it. I've got a police report here stating that Winston Alfred Ross committed suicide last night by jumping out of his sixth floor apartment window!"

Harry and Teri swapped a stunned look.

"Coincidence." Teri said.

"Can't be." Harry replied.

"But why kill himself?"

"Guilt."

Daphne's eyes welled up with tears.

Harry Kovac tried to reason with himself. His emotions were conflicted and definitely confused. Had his questions from yesterday driven Winston to take his own life? Had Winston feared that Harry had been getting too close to discovering some ill doing, that Winston had indeed sabotaged Zero Crane's car and the scientist couldn't live with the guilt?

The other question was: what was Winston Alfred Ross doing that he feared exposure by a pair of private investigators?

"He didn't look the suicidal type." Teri stated. "What I saw of him, at least. He seemed too much of a pussy to get the nerve up to kill himself." She shrugged. "Who knew."

"I agree." Harry said at length. "Nothing in his profile, nothing significant in his past, and certainly nothing in his appearance would immediately place him as a man capable of such self immolation. He had enough issues growing up that if he had ever considered it before he would've done it long ago, and the medical records which Daphne located would've indicated any underlying issues. His life was running its course without too much stress, at least that's the impression I got of him. He was too arrogant and disdainful, for one thing."

"Unless he couldn't live with killing my husband." Daphne Crane said in as matter-of-fact a voice as she could muster.

Harry wondered if Winston hadn't intended the act of killing. Maybe he had sabotaged the car out of irrational anger, regretted it, found out from Harry what had happened and that was enough to tip him over the edge. But as Harry recounted their conversation from yesterday in his mind he couldn't think of anything which Winston did to indicate that was a possibility. The man had tampered with Zero's car, that was obvious, but there had been no sign, no indication whatsoever, that he regretted that action.

What, then?

"Maybe that's it." Teri suggested. "He was tipped over the edge. Dare I say: by your visit."

"I wonder what his father will make of this news." Harry contemplated.

"The ex-politician who owns a village?" Daphne Crane said cynically. "Like he cares. They fell out years ago, according to the press. Money can't buy a happy family!"

Fatal Wealth and Hellbeing, indeed!

"So what do we do now, boss?" Teri asked.

Harry steepled his fingers and leant back in the chair, considering the options, mentally juggling their workload.

"We have to think practically," offered Daphne. "Stephen Smith is paying us a lot of money to follow through with this car thing, we can't neglect him despite… you know."

"Sure." Harry couldn't argue. "Teri, are you okay to pick up where I left off on the Smith job?"

Teri nodded, "No problem. Just give me all the details."

"Thank you." Daphne said.

"I'm going to find out everything I can about Winston Ross's suicide," Harry said thoughtfully, "just to be certain that's what it was."

"You're not convinced." Teri stated.

"No. And I don't know why. It's just a gut instinct thing, and my gut says something is wrong. I wish I could figure out what it is, but there we go." Harry stretched his arms. "Teri, this woman who Winston went to the Sunday school meeting with, whats her status?"

"Hard to tell, boss," Teri admitted. "Winston didn't seem overly thrilled when he picked her up from his home. In fact, the area where she lived in Plumstead seemed like somewhere a man like him wouldn't go, unless I'm just turning into a snob! But it didn't. The place where she lives is a brown brick mid-terrace house, probably built in the nineteen fifties. When they arrived at the meeting in Wroxham he held her hand, but even that seemed like an uncomfortable gesture. And he dropped her straight home afterwards."

Harry turned to Daphne, "Can you…?"

"Already on it." Came the reply.

"And can you also dig up as much information on The Sanctity of Sunday thing?"

Harry turned the flier over in his hand. It had the outward appearance of a tub-thumping money making scheme with little substance to back it up. Family Health and Wellbeing. On the surface alone this statement seemed very noble and worthy, and perhaps they attracted members of the general public who needed this connection. Often, though, these were schemers out to exploit and maybe arouse some controversy, however minor. They were more suited to the back-woods of American, Harry thought, wryly. A fanatical group of people whose work wasn't even on the periphery of interest to anyone important. But who knows, thought Harry. Some of these groups, these minor idealistic fanatics, had historically caused headline grabbing attention through their actions.

"Right," Harry said decisively, "no use sitting here!"

# CHAPTER SIXTEEN

Marti Baines was still on a thrilling high after last nights The Sanctity of Sunday meeting. The talk had aroused her slumbering mind like it usually did, awakening her from the work day drudgery. These meetings always produced the same galvanising effect for Marti, by presenting an impassioned new outlook on the world around her and how society can be lifted from its present doldrums - and her heart swelled with belief that she would be a part of the resurrection of humanity.

Today her work day would definitely be different. Within Marti was an inescapable air of release in her soul that was almost palpable.

It was like she had awakened from the best nights sleep ever, and Marti was already feeling a joyous skip in her step, a gaiety of mind, and a sense of deep purpose to help her colleagues by bringing a smile to their day.

A day-after glow from The Sanctity of Sunday meeting, alongside a renewed must try harder attitude - that had almost been a life motto for Marti.

She was forty-six years of age, although her friend Alfie had told her to claim to be age neutral, which made her laugh because in this society one's self-options had reached ludicrous parody. For goodness sake, Marti told herself, I'm not past my prime yet!

The endless drudgery of cleaning had kept her feeling physically quite fit and reasonably healthy. Marti had avoided every COVID symptom and had, wisely as it turned out, not been vaccinated like the majority of the global population. She hadn't even had a cold!

Supposedly this was middle-age. Judgemental society categorised her as past her prime, but that was utter nonsense. Ridiculous! Maybe it had taken all these years of people looking down from their high perches at Marti, what with the let downs and rejections and humdrum existence - which was all they saw. Yet for Marti, finally now was the time to realise her own potential and it certainly was not too late.

Marti was indeed counting her blessings this morning.

Today of all days, when she and Alfie would be affecting change for herself and the country.

The influence should be overwhelming.

Her mind should be whirling.

She shouldn't be so calm.

Marti had known Alfie Ross for just six months but in that time his friendship had expanded her mind by introducing her to new possibilities and ideas. Alfie made her feel like she had never had a life before meeting him, as though she had always known him. Maybe in some esoteric level she had always known him, which Marti most definitely believed. Alfie had brought her to The Sanctity of Sunday meetings and her mind was indeed blown. She had been cynical at first, believing that anyone who preached so fervently was perhaps a nutcase, their followers on some type of mind control drug. Marti had seen their kind on television. They drew the needy into their circle, the lost souls who could see no hope or purpose to their own lives, brain-washing them with an idea to send them off on some quest which inevitably went badly.

Not Alfie. Not Marti. And certainly not The Sanctity of Sunday followers.

Marti didn't need resurrection. She wasn't a lost cause. She had been content to live life her way, on her own terms, and she was happier now than she'd ever been. Life had been shit to her! Marti had experienced marriage to a man who cheated on her, took all her money, put her down at every opportunity until she decided that enough was enough and finished with him. This was done under her own volition, without outside influence, so that proved how strong she was.

Twenty years ago to the day she had divorced the man, freed herself from servitude to a symbol, an old-fashioned concept which people had urged her towards. But she defied everything and everyone, set out on her own, defined her own destiny, and was a better person for it. Sure, she didn't perhaps socialise much and kept herself to herself at work, but what was wrong with that? Absolutely nothing.

Twenty years on from those wasteful, hurtful times, Marti had her cats, her job, her home, her friendship with Alfie, and purpose in life.

There was nothing romantic between she and Alfie. They were friends. What was wrong with that? Can't a man and women just be friends? Alfie held her hand last night because he was excited about the meeting, and no doubt today also. Marti was sure, despite the quickening in her heart, that romance wasn't an option. His eyes had been brighter, yes, but they had just held hands. That was all. There was no sense of intimacy. It was stupid to think otherwise. Marti was happy with a friendship. Why shouldn't she be?

"Good morning, Pat!" Marti said cheerily to Pat, one of her work colleagues.

They were in the janitors room which all the cleaners at Sunny Shades Holiday Park shared.

Sunny Shades was an eco-friendly park set amidst woodland and heathland with static holiday homes and spaces for tourers. It's grounds included trails for walking and cycling, plus an indoor swimming pool and gym, restaurants, an entertainment club and small supermarket. It was a popular destination for those wishing a complete wind-down from the hubbub of life, or to experience the outdoor life, and there were plenty of activities for everyone either on site or off. July and August were peak seasons so the cleaners were kept especially busy right now.

"Good morning." Pat replied, a split-second pause to study Marti who was, by her own admission, often aloof and unapproachable. But not today. "How are you today, Marti? It's a lovely morning."

"It certainly is." Marti agreed. "I might take a walk around the heath after work. I don't believe I've ever had the opportunity at this time of year, it's always so busy."

"It is that." Pat replied, as she finished filling her cleaning trolley and headed for the door, "Fancy a coffee at break time?"

"That sounds lovely." Marti replied, surprising herself by the positivity in her voice. "Why not."

Pat gave a little acknowledgment incline to her head, smiled, and left the closet.

Marti tied the smock about her waist, which had Sunny Shades and it's leafy logo embroidered upon it, for the final time.

Freedom from servitude.

It had been Alfie's suggestion, really, although Marti admittedly had often wondered about the prospect of becoming her own boss one day. She already had a good client base to formally run her own cleaning services. It would mean working similar hours than she was used to but the rewards would be greater. It had only been uncertainty which had held her back. The risk involved tied Marti's stomach in knots. But with Alfie's support, she was confident it would be worth it in the longterm.

Obviously none of her colleagues had been made aware of her decision yet, she had clearly stated to her boss that she wanted secrecy in the matter. There had been no motive behind her request, really, because she never talked to or socialised with anybody she worked with, so they probably wouldn't care or even notice if she were no longer there.

Maybe Marti would tell Pat later.

Maybe not.

Marti sorted out her cleaning materials, diluted the business-approved eco-friendly detergent solution which was harmless to the environment and humans.

At least it had been harmful before today.

Alfie had told her the vial of liquid he had given her last night, and the contents of which she now mixed with the detergent, was a pathogen much like the covid virus had been. He had assured her that it wasn't harmful. Much like covid it had been manufactured in a laboratory to cause influenza like-symptoms which could spread easily and quickly between people, and create a new pandemic. Alfie had discussed the idea with her for weeks, saying that the government and society needed another kick up the backside to shake free of the societal ennui. Much like The Sanctity of Sunday speaker espoused passionately yesterday. It was as if Alfie had known in advance that this was to be the topic the night before his plan was to be carried out.

A happy coincidence, so far as Marti was concerned.

Prepared for her wonderful day ahead and with a noticeable spring to her step, Marti joyously set to her last day of employment at Sunny Shades Holiday Park.

## CHAPTER SEVENTEEN

"We have officially recorded Winston Alfred Ross's death as suicide." DCI Gnanakaran stated.

Harry Kovac acknowledged this information with a smile and a nod.

They were standing outside the quadrangle of Riverside apartments, a luxury complex whose monthly rental cost Harry didn't want to contemplate. These were definitely apartments for affluent working professionals. They are well maintained and desirable, yet on closer inspection the lack of security cameras was a bizarre omission. The Riverside entertainment complex in Norwich was quite fashionable and constantly bustling with people. There were numerous fish-eye cameras dotted throughout, connected to a central location, yet nothing directly outside this set of apartments - what was it about this lack of surveillance recently? This had been an unforgivable oversight and undoubtedly as a consequence of this incident there would be a review on this point.

The crime scene itself, namely Winston's apartment, was cordoned off and Harry wasn't permitted entry despite his private investigator credentials. He was able to see the open window and Winston's final resting place, which had been surrounded by a cordon where forensics had scoured the brick-weave ground. The body of Winston had been removed to the morgue for a full post-mortem.

Harry looked upward at the window, thoughtfully, and not without frustration. He really could do with gaining access to the apartment, because an open window six storeys up yielded no clues from this distance. But Harry knew that procedures and protocols must be followed to the letter, he had been a barrier to private detectives himself when he was a police officer, so knew the score.

"How about unofficially?" Harry asked DCI Gnanakaran.

"Unofficially... Between you and I." The DCI added that last part unnecessarily. "The victim was naked when he jumped and there's signs in the apartment that he had... probably entertained a guest. There's signs of sexual activity having taken place, and alcohol consumption," the DCI shrugged, "not that that's anything usual. There are no obvious signs of a struggle, at least not a violent struggle, and Winston Ross doesn't appear to have suffered any injury apart from the ones caused by his fall."

"And there are no witnesses?" Harry asked.

"None."

"And nobody heard him fall?"

"No. The rooms are very well insulated from outside noises, so none of his neighbours would've been aware of anything untoward."

"No surveillance cameras, I noticed."

"That'll change after this."

Harry agreed, "None of the businesses have this property in sight, I suppose?"

"Unfortunately not."

Harry snorted derisively, "Seems like a really shoddy planning oversight."

"I agree, Harry. The rent on these apartments is astronomical. They even have access to a private underground car park. You'd think surveillance cameras would be obvious. Which is one of the reasons why the possibility that this was murder hasn't been ruled out."

"Hmm," Harry mumbled. "Well, that's not for us to deal with, I guess. Has his father been told the official and unofficial report?"

"Par for the course. His Dad's still fair game for newsworthy scandals."

"Fair enough. Anyway, thanks for telling me what you can, it's most appreciated."

"Hope it helps."

"Sure it does."

"And if you unearth anything useful…"

"I'll let you know straight away."

With that, Harry walked back to his car. His visit had yielded more results than he could've anticipated. He hadn't expected anyone at the crime scene to know who he was, so it had been fortuitous that DCI Gnanakaran had been present. Most of all, she had been helpful. The potential nature of Winston Ross's death had been held back from the media while an investigation took place.

The question was, if it wasn't suicide, who killed him and why? Was it a spur of the moment sex crime? Or was is connected to anything which Zero and Harry had stumbled upon?

Harry drove back to the office, which took just ten minutes, and found Daphne at her desk crying. She composed herself, apologised to Harry who told her there was no need to say sorry.

"I found everything you asked for, Harry." Daphne said, sniffing. "It's on your laptop."

"Thanks, Daphne. Have you heard from Teri, at all?"

"Not yet."

"Okay. Look…why don't you go home to your parents, get out of here, there must be something else you could be doing under the circumstances. All your work is done here and I'm not going anywhere just yet. Should we get any clients turn up I can see to them myself."

Daphne looked hesitantly through glazed eyes, her bottom lip quivering. Eventually she nodded, wiped her eyes, gathered her stuff and departed the office with a tentative thank you.

The office seemed abruptly silent. The ambient whirring of the computer fan ran softly. The gentle, rhythmic ticking of the clock from Zero's office seemed like a mournful reminder of his passing.

Harry's heart suddenly felt heavy. Life had been removed from this environment. He would sorely miss Zero's jovial presence, as would Daphne, of course. Her strength was a shining example of courage. Se-ri was still in Scotland on business, and wouldn't be back for another few days, her absence leaving a hole in his world.

Not one for lengthy morbid rumination, Harry pulled himself together, made a strong coffee - caffeine was the only drug which worked on him, it galvanised him into action - and went into his office. First thing he did was put in his earbuds and connect the Bluetooth to his phone, playing some random seventies music station on low.

Opening up his laptop the first file he found was on Marti Baines, the woman with whom Winston Ross was acquainted. The information was garnered from social services, the DVLA - it appeared her driving license had expired - and work records. There was scant evidence that she led the kind of life which would appeal to a PHD scientist such as Winston. The facts contained nothing much more than her date of birth, her relationship status, financial situation, qualifications and a head-and-shoulders photograph taken about ten years ago. Marti appeared quite plain, not that official photography offered anything remotely glamorous about them. She had no debts and no dependents - a divorce twenty years ago.

It all appeared quite innocuous. Marti was an average woman making her way in life by dotting her 'I's' and crossing her 'T's' like a good citizen. But the information told Harry very little about her character except that she was independent. Marti was possibly cynical around relationships owing to the divorce, which gave credence to the fact that her and Winston were just good friends.

But how?

Their worlds were the polar opposite.

How did Winston and Marti meet?

Harry shrugged; was this really significant to anything pertaining to Winston's death? Probably not. But maybe she could offer some insight into the man.

Next, Harry opened up the figuratively hefty file which Daphne had compiled on The Sanctity of Sunday group.

It read like Harry expected; as a highly flamboyant promotional propaganda statement, although some of it made sense fundamentally. 'Emerge from your state imposed shell', it said, 'and listen to the power of freedom.' Which was a pretty vague declaration, but most of the diatribe which Harry saw consisted of similar member baiting stuff. Rousing was the order of their manifesto, much like that of a political party or evangelical movement. Strength in unity, and all that. They offered to open the mind to family values bettering isolationism; consumers taking control of their corporate choices; opening eyes to the world around them.

The main aim of The Sanctity of Sunday was all too self-explanatory, and Harry thought back to his earlier chat with Daphne and Teri about its pros, cons and realistic outcome. Yes, the idea sounded wonderful, but there were too many business factors to take into account that made it unachievable. Unfortunately in this cynical world where conglomerates rule there was no way whatsoever that any Government would sanction a total Sunday shutdown, just so family and friends could enjoy time together. Who wanted that to happen, when shopping was far better!

Although during the long forgotten, forever lingering, pandemic where the NHS and Supermarket workers had been heroes, businesses were forced into lockdown. If it had lasted a day, most people would have coped. They would've enjoyed family time. But the duration became a financial and personal strain which affects us even today.

People like Winston Ross worked hard during those times. Had the strain been too much?

Harry sighed, wondering how a man like Winston, a man who shunned personal interaction, a man of intellect and scientific logic, would be at all associated with a group extolling the virtues of family and friendship.

That was until, he saw who the Chief Executive of the organisation was: Winston's father, Lambert Ross.

This made everything fall neatly into place for Harry. It meant that Winston Ross wasn't as estranged from his father as he had led everyone to believe, because why attend something when you were strongly against the founder?

It still didn't answer half of the questions which Harry had. In fact, nothing which Harry was investigating had been explained yet pieces of the puzzle were coming together, forming a broken picture.

Harry sipped thoughtfully at his coffee. He wondered what Lambert Ross would make of the suicide of his son, would he face the press?

Picking up his smartphone, Harry opened the address book application and scrolled down to Begona Lec, a political journalist friend from way back when he was a London police officer. He hadn't spoken to Begona in a while, except for the occasional text message.

Harry phoned her and waited, and waited, until the call went to voicemail. He left her a brief message and asked her to call him back, then hung up. She was a busy person.

Harry went back to the files, specifically that of Winston's companion from yesterday, Marti Baines. According to her employment records she worked at the Sunny Shades Holiday Park, in Sheringham. This was their busy summer season, which meant she was bound to be there, so Harry decided to pay the place a visit.

## CHAPTER EIGHTEEN

Sunny Shades Holiday Park is three-hundred and fifty acres of woodland and green spaces, with a mixture of eco-friendly static holiday homes and designated sites for tourers. With its many miles of cycling and walking routes on or around the property, and nestled amidst undulating countryside, the award winning park attracts visitors from far and wide who desire a relaxing and stress free environment.

Harry hadn't been aware of the park, which was a mile east of the seaside destination of Sheringham, until he had carried out a web search. It looked very inviting, and upon his arrival by car at the entrance to the driveway, Harry realised that he hadn't even ventured to this part of Norfolk before now. He wondered how many people failed to explore their own country, and Harry considered that perhaps The Sanctity of Sunday wasn't such a bad idea after all. But this is what holiday time is for, surely? You work hard for time away with family, maybe a weekend with friends. There was no need to shut the entire country down for a day.

Or was there?

Harry drove slowly along the tree-lined driveway, adhering to the requested ten-miles per hour limit, which also proclaimed that 'Your Tranquil Getaway Ahead' and 'Now is the Time to Relax'. He saw a few helmeted cyclists amongst the trees, and the occasional isolated log cabin, giving the very impression which the park set out to achieve, of oneness with the natural environment. It was all very peaceful and stress free, like it's website claimed.

Parking up in the unmade car park, Harry was greeted by a delightful freshness to the shaded air. He had expected to notice the heat more, having had the cars air-conditioning on, with the external midday temperature registering twenty-eight degrees. But no, it was very pleasant amongst the trees.

The guests and visitors to the park consisted of all shapes and sizes, ages and genders, but all were dressed appropriately for this lovely summers day. In fact, Harry in his smart white shirt, dark grey chinos and lace-up genuine leather shoes seemed markedly out of place, like he was here on business rather than pleasure. This of course was precisely the image Harry intended.

Easily locating the oak leaf motif fronted reception building, Harry strode up to the desk and was greeted by an enthusiastic looking man in his mid-twenties, wearing the parks uniform and a name badge which told everyone that he was called 'Harvey the Hedgehog,' his gel-spiked hair lending credence to the moniker.

"Good," Harvey delightedly checked the clock on the wall beside him, "afternoon."

"Hello. And how are you today, Harvey?"

"Very well, thank you, sir. Lovely day."

"It is that, the weathers perfect. I bet you're busy?"

"We certainly are. How can I help?"

"I'm hoping you can," Harry said convivially. He showed Harvey his Private Investigator credentials. "There's nothing to worry about, Harvey," he put the younger man's instant concern to rest, "I'm interested in having a few words with one if your cleaners, a Miss Marti Baines, if that's possible. Basically, a friend of hers has been in an accident and my client has asked that I should see her to break the news."

"Oh, um, sure, no problem whatsoever." Harvey said without hesitation.

There was none of the bureaucratic hassle which Harry had anticipated.

"Thank you. I appreciate that. I'll try not to take her away from her work long, she must be incredibly busy."

Harvey nodded, but smiled, the perfect face to this relaxed environment. Harry could see that he was the model employee and a credit to the park, maybe he was relatively inexperienced and eager to please. The younger man checked his computer screen, tapped out a few commands, and nodded to himself.

"Would you like me to-?" Harvey trailed off, clearly hoping that Harry wouldn't need to be escorted to Marti's location on the park.

"No, no, I'll be just fine. If you can tell me where I can find her on the park, I'll leave you to your work."

"Thank you." Relief swept over Harvey's face. He handed Harry a map of the park, pointed to a spot upon it, and gave directions.

"Thank you very much, Harvey." Harry said with a smile, taking the proffered map.

"You're welcome."

"Have a great day."

Harvey grinned.

Harry went in his way, thinking that it had been far easier to garner the information he had required than he had anticipated. Harvey lacked the experience which made a person cynical, took away the gullibility, and made them less ingratiating. The barriers to Harry's profession.

The park's 'Village Square' teemed with life. Young people played outdoor table tennis; children laughed gaily as they were swung by parents on the jungle equipment for juveniles; adults sat and drank or ate and chatted; a mature couple played boules; splashes could be heard from an unseen swimming pool; while myriad other people passed through, going to or from their next point of interest. The smell of various cooking food wafted pleasantly through the air. It really was a very pleasing environment away from the hustle and bustle of town or city life, and one to relax by with not a frown in sight.

Harry avoided the people, skirted the square, not wishing to attract attention to himself because presently he most definitely did not fit into this holiday vibe.

Finding the area of the park where he could expect to find Marti Baines was easy enough, and there were fewer tourists about the log cabins, people choosing to venture out at this time of day, which obviously worked in Harry's favour.

Harry saw Marti Baines immediately. Her face was unmistakably the one which was upon the DVLA records despite it being ten years out of date. She hadn't altered a great deal save a darker caste to her skin. Marti had been fundamentally a person who had never looked young, at least that's the impression Harry was gathering. She was stooped over her cleaning trolley, but not in the hunched manner of a person drained and altered by their job. Marti's posture was good, and her figure was lived-in but not through excessive consumption. And she was whistling quite happily to herself, which made Harry feel like a heel for the news he was about to impart.

Marti must have instinctively sensed his presence because she turned around to face him before Harry had the opportunity to attract her attention. She regarded his appearance and soon assessed that he wasn't a guest of the park. Her whistling stopped, the jollity she was feeling slipped instantly off her face.

Harry felt sorry for her straight away.

"Good afternoon." Harry said in a tone which didn't intimidate. "Marti Baines?"

Marti hesitantly replied, "Yes."

"Sorry to interrupt you," Harry said, and produced his official identification, which he showed her.

Marti's face paled instantly. She gulped. It was the reaction of a unusually timid, introverted personality, when they are faced with officialdom and they feel unnecessarily guilty. And panicked guilt was all over Marti's face. Harry was more than accustomed to such a reaction. Some people couldn't help their response, there was nothing they could do to avoid it, innocent or not, it was a chemical reaction.

"It's about Winston Ross." Harry said.

A flicker of initial confusion upon Marti's face was soon replaced by an utter dread. Harry thought she was going to pass out. Her eyes grew larger in fright, they welled up with tears, her lower lip quivered.

Harry felt terribly sorry for her. This woman had no idea what was coming but could obviously sense the seriousness, why else would a private investigator be here, today? Poor woman.

Marti stuttered and stammered unintelligibly, then finally found some modicum of composure, "Oh no!" Was all she could say before dropping to her knees and crying into her hands.

This definitely was not the reaction which Harry had anticipated, but he had many years of experience to draw upon so was unswerving from his aim. He looked at this broken woman who hadn't even been told what had happened yet. Her reaction might be extreme, to say the least, but in this age which we live in where mental health issues are rife, Harry wasn't taking anything for granted. He certainly didn't want to tip her over the edge, especially as she had seemed so utterly cheerful when he first set eyes on her.

"He was a good friend?" Harry gently nudged her back into the moment.

Marti looked up at him through teary eyes, snot trailing into her wet mouth. She blinked. A big mournful sigh expelled itself from between her lips. Her body shuddered.

"I'm...I'm sorry..." Marti said.

"That should be my line." Harry offered with a consoling smile.

The expressions on Marti's face changed from terrified to confused to dread to confused on a cyclical basis, as if she was gradually absorbing the words and meaning being spoken to her.

"Alfie..." she gulped with palpable, panicked breathlessness, "...Alfie..."

Harry nodded, "Yes, I'm sorry, but Alfie has gone."

It was if a sledgehammer blow had been dealt to Marti. Her face twisted with utter despair, but the opposite to before, Harry noted. It was as if this wasn't the news which Marti had been expecting. As if she had somehow been anticipating Harry's purpose differently. Clearly Marti was shaken by the news of Winston Ross's death, that was most definite, yet earlier her reaction was based on something other than the possibility of this information. This was a reaction more than the sum of its parts. Marti was fairly besotted by Winston, yet their friendship jarred awkwardly in Harry's minds eye, because they couldn't possibly be more disparate humans, living in totally different worlds.

"Alfie is dead?" Marti said, her composure flimsy but returning to a more natural tone.

"That's right."

"Oh. Alfie."

"But that's not why you thought I was here." Harry stated. "Was it, Marti?"

She tried to avert her eyes. Now she looked positively guilty once more, unable to hide the truth.

"Why did you think I was here, Marti.?" Harry probed with composed directness. Had Winston told her about his actions against Zero Crane?

Marti cast a furtive glance at her work trolley, before resolving to stare at her hands, breaking down in tears once again, sobbing uncontrollably. Harry wondered if this conversation could actually proceed any further. Not only was Marti worried about him, but she was now clearly becoming concerned for her job. This woman was in such a state that she was likely to have a complete nervous breakdown in front of him, and however much he desired to learn the facts from Marti, and what it is she is concealing he couldn't be the initiator of her down fall.

Now was the time to strike, though. While this woman was at her lowest, her most susceptible. There was no time for Harry to let feelings of compassion rule. He needed to find out the truth.

"What's going on, Marti?" Harry prompted in a voice which snapped her to attention. "What has Alfie done?"

Marti's wide, frightened eyes looked up at Harry as he loomed threateningly over her. She shook her head pitifully. Harry didn't feel good about himself right there and then, but sometimes emotions had to be buried.

"Alfie...told me this was for the good of society." Marti sobbed. "Like our meetings. Poor Alfie."

"The Sanctity of Sundays?" Harry prompted.

Marti nodded, not questioning his knowledge, "Alfie said it would bring people together. Like the last Pandemic. People need to be reminded how important family is. The corporations need fixing."

"What are you talking about? What has Alfie done?"

Marti's eyes flitted to her washer bucket, "My Alfie created a new virus, see?"

Instinctively Harry backed away, eying the bucket and the woman with trepidation. He pulled out his phone and immediately dialled the number for DCI Gnanakaran, filling her in on the details of his findings at Sunny Shades Holiday Park, and the importance that she act with due alacrity, before hanging up and returning his attention to Marti Baines.

"How many holiday homes have you cleaned today?" Harry asked. She hesitated. "Look. Marti. People's lives depend on your information. How many holiday homes have you cleaned?" He repeated forcefully.

"Six." Marti answered, terrified now.

"Okay. Go and get a park supervisor. Now!"

Marti was shook from her self pitying torpor by the authority in Harry's voice, scuttling off to see to his command. Harry eyed the bucket suspiciously, wondering what kind of chemical Winston Ross had developed.

Harry's smartphone purred almost seductively in his pocket. It was Begona Lec.

"Hey, Kovac!" She said playfully, her voice a bright uplifting lilt after the subdued conversation which Harry had just had with Marti, and doom-laden consequences. "How's the exciting world of the P.I.?"

"Hey, Begona." Harry replied. "It's pretty good. How are the scandals with you?"

Begona laughed, "The usual philandering and cheating, you know? The sort of stuff you small town gumshoes deal with all the time, only I'm reporting on the big boy stuff."

"Aye, we country folk don't know the half of it, I'm sure." Harry looked once more at the potentially deadly chemical filled bucket.

"You sure don't. I could make your toes curl literally if you only knew half the stuff I've got on record at the moment. Anyway, what's this stuff about Lambert Ross's boy? You been investigating him, or what?"

"Kind of, Begona, kind of." Harry told her a few of the pertinent details in the concise form which she appreciated, omitting his latest discovery.

Begona emitted a low whistle, "Sounds juicy. Look, Kovac, you're in luck. I'm in London at the moment, so I can help you out. How about I get myself invited to Ross's announcement he's making tomorrow? Not that I'd need an invite, it's an open-mike show at the town hall in the village next to his... I presume you already looked into Lambert? He practically owns a village, which isn't unknown for landed gentry, of course, but in his case it's detrimental to one's health!"

"I did not know that."

"Kovac, you surprise me! I thought you'd have brushed up on all the pertinent facts!"

"Evidently there's a gap in my knowledge."

"Never mind. Brush up before you come along, because I presume that's your intention?"

"Sure. Why not." Harry said, thinking that it might be more significant an announcement than he might've anticipated. "I've nothing better to do."

"Great," Begona said. "See you there tomorrow."

And without further ado the line went dead.

Harry grinned bleakly to himself. He had more research to do, not least the time and location of Lambert Ross's announcement to the press. But first of all there was small matter of putting Winston Ross's chemical plot in the hands of the police before it got out of control.

# CHAPTER NINETEEN

Early next morning Harry was driving unhurriedly toward his destination of Bramfield, south of the privately owned Richton Village, nestled in the deep Hertfordshire countryside. It was a journey of about two and a half hours. The music station on his DAB radio played a mixture of seventies and eighties tunes spliced with DJ witticisms and interspersed by frequent travel bulletins and news summaries. These suited the journey, they kept part of Harry's mind on the road while the other half processed the details which he had garnered from an internet search on the ex-politician, Lambert Ross, whose son had died in a suspiciously contrived suicide. At least this was Harry's opinion, maybe compounded by the details which Marti Baines had imparted. Winston Ross had much to feel guilty about so suicide maybe was his escape.

DCI Gnanakaran would keep him informed as best she could, while Sunny Shades Holiday Park had been locked down, while containment of the chemical which Winston Ross had developed and Marti Baines deployed was ongoing.

Lambert was due to make a speech at Bramfield Village Hall for the media at around noon.

Lambert Henry Ross had been born into money and could be justifiably described as landed gentry. Richton Hall was the ancestral home handed down through generations of his family - and after the death of Winston Alfred, it would now pass onto the youngest son, upon Lambert's death, Willoughby Charles. Such was the vast sprawl of the estate, Richton Village sprang into existence during the late eighteen hundreds, with many of the original buildings intact which brought tourists to them. Now, the village of forty period homes boasted an exquisite public house, a fashionable boutique cafe, three small retailers selling plush items, and a field which had been converted into a gravel car park set at the rear, hiding it from the high street so it didn't encroach on the olde world picturesque quality of the village. Not a single satellite dish was on show!

The present landlord of Richton Hall had inherited the estate upon the passing of his father, the famous doctor and politician, Sir Archibald Michael Ross, who had been a friend and confidante of Sir Winston Churchill during and after the Second World War. During his thirty-plus year tenure, Lambert Ross had altered nothing externally, just adding a few of his own personal proclivities to the private interior rooms of the hall, away from the probing eyes of the visiting general public.

Lambert Ross followed the very traditionalist childhood of the establishment: a nursemaid, nanny, private education, exclusive higher education, then military service. A path not unlike his father. He served in the Falklands conflict after which he was publicly honoured.

Upon his discharge Lambert married a young socialite who was with his first child, Winston Alfred, and they spent a year at Richton Hall, time for the young man to consider his options and conceive a second child, a girl - who died aged two of meningitis- while a third would follow five years later after the first of Lambert Ross's extra-marital dalliances. Lambert studied the political scene on the metaphorical arm of his father, gaining some backers who supported his ideas when he father passed away. Lambert's PR firm played up the grief of this young man and he become one of the youngest members of Parliament to hold a constituency.

Lambert's background and upbringing brought with it certain views on the ever shrinking global importance of England as an island nation, as the country became more absorbed by the EU's economic development. Unlike his father before him, who had wholeheartedly embraced change, Lambert reared up against these new realities and argued strongly against the government promoting them. To assert his Englishness and that of his estate he imbued the traditional values and practices which he believed were long forgotten and overdue a reappraisal. Lambert feared the country's history would be utterly destroyed if the English people were not allowed to live those traditions, and were forced to forego them for fear of being branded as racist.

The major political parties took Lambert Ross for a lunatic who couldn't adapt to the rapid changes in society and the infrastructure of the country. Forced to represent the Liberal's, and gaining a vast populist following amongst those who saw themselves as true English citizens, he continued to propose radical reforms and challenges to his opposition which bordered on fanaticism. Upon his nomination as Liberal leader, which he held through three years, he ran for Prime Minister but failed. He was ousted from the Leadership position after a controversial accusation of rape by a minor, followed by a string of similar allegations brought against him.

Exonerated, Lambert Ross left public service five years ago, residing at Richton Hall, with certain antics occasionally swerving him into the sights of the media and politics, while his views and quaint English values were frequently mocked by some critics.

The village of Bramfield which bordered Richton Village to its south, was easy enough for Harry to locate without resorting to satnav. Most of the residences sat either side of the main road, plus a few businesses, on the uniquely named Main Road! It seemed tidy, gardens were in bloom, and there were a minimal amount of new builds. Effectively it bore a distinct resemblance to the smaller villages in Norfolk, or anywhere else in the country with a low population, for that matter.

Harry Kovac was soon parked in the loose-gravel car park of the Red Stag Inn, itself situated on the northern apex of Gobions Lane and Bramfield Road, opposite the Village Hall. He had already noticed the sigh pointing northwards for Richton Village And Hall, two miles.

A media presence was already setting itself up for the arrival of Lambert Ross. Some reporters could be seen wandering and chatting to locals or amongst their own ilk.

Harry's friend Begona Lec, the London political journalist, was already awaiting him beside her car, a shiny new-plate Audi. She was ten years younger than Harry, full of agency, enthusiastic, and knowledgeable about the world today. A smartphone was seemingly glued permanently to her right hand, and a Bluetooth earpiece was visible in her left ear.

They exchanged friendly pleasantries when finally Begona finished her call.

"So who is she!" Begona asked pointedly.

"Her name is Parisa Dane." Harry said. "Is it that obvious I'm seeing someone?"

"Sure. It's been, what, over a year since I last saw you and you have a…glowing radiance about you."

"It might've been the air-con!"

"Na. I know you. I'm happy for you."

"Thanks."

She led and Harry followed behind, across the gravel, catching up with her roadside.

"Quite the turnout." Begona commented. "Should be an interesting circus. The villagers here are not fans of Lambert Ross. They consider him a usurper, I guess, despite his thirty year residency as lord of the manor." She sniggered. "Most of his supporters will be bussed in from Richton or otherwise from far and wide. Might be a few heated clashes, if we're lucky." She nodded in the direction of a specific national media service van not known for their reporting subtlety. "That's what they're hoping for. And probably Ross himself, too. Let's face it, well placed and timed controversy never harmed anyone."

"Are they expecting Lambert Ross to announce his return to the political arena, then?" Harry asked.

"You can bank on it. His sons suicide couldn't be more perfectly timed. Ross shows some grief, gives a brief speech, if we're lucky, about the injustices in the world and what he would do to correct them if he were in power. Bring up the increasing suicide statistics which, I might add, make for shocking reading. Throw in a few printable Everyman soundbites to make him seem like a normal guy wanting normal changes, rather than self-promotion. There's an election coming up. Who could resist it? I guarantee you this is already being spun by his PR team and they're creating the aftershock."

Harry nodded sagely, "And past transgressions be damned."

"Just grist for the mill for the tabloids. Never harmed anyone with enough money and power. You don't have to look to far in the past for examples." Begona turned to Harry, looked him in eye. "So what's your angle? What's a

Private Eye got to do with Lambert Ross, or have you already told me everything?"

Harry sketched out a few more of the details from his interview with Winston Alfred Ross, including the death of Zero Crane, and yesterday's reaction from Marti Baines - still omitting her admission, not because Harry didn't trust Begona's discretion, but the seriousness of the event prevented full disclosure.

"I'm not entirely certain what I'm hoping to learn here," Harry admitted. "But the son wasn't as disowned by the father as one might be led to believe. I cannot say why or how, at least not yet, because I'm not entirely certain there's anything to report but...well, you can break the story if there's to be one."

"Jeez, thanks." Begona acknowledged without hesitation or malice.

"The son was a piece of work, I've established that, but if he was doing that work alone or at the bidding of his father, that's something I intend finding out." He shrugged. "I don't know. Maybe I'm clutching at transparent straws."

Harry and Begona were observing a heated argument taking place across the road from the Inn between two middle-aged men. It was a slagging match about whose views and convictions were the right ones. The gist was easy to follow because of the political nature of the events which were soon to be upon them, a powder keg, one might say. One man thought it slanderous that his opponent should object to Lambert Ross giving his address in Bramfield, and not from his own lofty fiefdom, while the other was defending the decision.

"You thought the son was a piece of work." Begona said. "Wait till to see dad! There are not many bigoted men left in this land, especially those who are proud of their bigotry, but Lambert Ross is certainly one of the few. It'll be interesting to find out how he is going to spin anything positive!"

"His son didn't fall far from the family tree, that much is for sure."

A reporter with a smartphone, to record the fracas for posterity, approached the two men who squabbled like children, or backbenchers. This reporter was somehow able to deflect the argument from the duo into a sensible conversation about what they thought was wrong, and right, with the situation its implications, and if they wouldn't mind being quoted by the reporter.

"This is why they call it a circus! Full of terrifyingly unfunny clowns."

"Are those two for real?" Harry asked.

Begona studied the two men arguing their individual points with the reporter.

"They're very professional actors, if it's a put up." Begona said. "But I wouldn't put it past Ross's team to concoct a stunt like this. Certainly wouldn't be the first time. They're not called spin-doctors without reason."

Harry and Begona crossed Main Road to the footpath, stepping over the low metal partition which separated it from the Village Hall grassed car park. The building was a typical village hall building with what looked like a bowling green abutting its southern edge.

Begona nodded a greeting to a couple of reporters who she obviously knew from the business.

'Should be a show." Begona said.

"Ross is gonna announce he's running again." One of the reporters stated that which Begona had already suggested, which seemed the all round consensus.

"I heard he's grief stricken by what happened to his son." The second reporter said flippantly.

"I heard he offed him for the publicity value!" Said the other jokingly.

"He's going for a coalition." The second one said. "Liberal and Looney Left."

"We'll find out soon enough." An eavesdropping journalist piped up, nodding in the direction of Bramfield Road, from which emerged a mini-bus followed by a classic black English coach-built open-topped motorcar from the nineteen forties, which was part of a private collection owned by Ross himself, with small flags of St. George fluttering atop the front fenders of both. The car was a statement in and of itself. It showed Lambert Ross to be proudly traditional and, unfortunately, pretentious.

From half-way along Main Road a throng of people started to march in their direction. Harry supposed they were local residents resistant to what was about was to transpire, the kind of ever-present protestors who always turned out for this kind of event - probably carrying rotten tomatoes in their knitting bags. Whenever there was a chance of media exposure you could guarantee a good, organised turn out, placards and all.

Harry estimated that upward of two-hundred people had turned out, which seemed a far greater number considering the relatively small street. Amongst the mixture of people were a few anomalies standing out in Harry's eye: a long-haired, leather-clad biker baring a resemblance to Gandalf; a nurse in uniform with an angry, forlorn expression; a couple formally dressed bearing Union Jack flags. They couldn't be more disparate and separate from the conservatively dressed masses.

"Quite the circus." Begona reiterated her earlier comment, watching the gathering throng. "One way or the other this little event, whatever Ross's statement is to be, will thrust him back into the spotlight. Just like he wants, for better or worse. I wonder what his actual agenda will be. He can't return with the same focus as last time. The political climate has moved on even further after his five years away. Ross will know that, of course, and his PR team, his financial partners and co-conspirators will be well aware of that, but if they're to succeed they need to usher a complete turnaround for their man. Either way, they're going to have to put a boot into a real hornets nest!" Begona grinned and shrugged with obvious cynicism, "Alternatively, this is just going to be a father showing grief over his sons suicide."

Harry remained noncommittal. He had lost faith in political mechanisations many years ago. In his job with Scotland Yard he had become disillusioned from constantly banging his head against a wall of bureaucracy, mostly from those who were self-serving power hungry politicians trying to further their own agenda, tying the hands of the chain of command. Harry knew from experience the number of rich and powerful people who had covered up their follies, pretending to be humbled by their transgressions, apologising yet continuing on their merry way. Lambert Ross would just be joining a long line of fallen self-entitled men warmly welcomed back to the fold by their slathering brethren.

# CHAPTER TWENTY

When Lambert Ross emerged from his car he sported the most fake humble expression Harry had ever seen. It was ludicrous, yet the public, his public, lapped it up. The reborn politician waved gratefully to those who had turned out for him, beaming a hundred-watt smile, while deferentially acknowledging his cheering devotees and pretending to completely ignore the jeers. The whole event was so stage managed that Harry had to laugh. The circus had definitely entered town!

Lambert Ross had recently turned sixty-five. His dyed black hair was slicked down with oil, cut into a basin style with a centre parting, making him resemble a particular early twentieth century German politician, sans moustache. His unblemished face and clear brown eyes did effectively make him look ten-years younger, as did his relatively fit six-feet four inches frame, a point of fact he took pride in because the stresses and strains of life should have made him look his age, or older. Lambert's skin was healthily tanned owing to his outdoor lifestyle and travelling. Clearly the man oozed high-born charisma and potent vitality, but his features also presented the self righteous arrogance of a man who believed himself better than anyone else. Lambert was landed gentry from old school money, a privileged Englishman whose vast wealth and power meant he was accustomed to being the top dog - which made his fall from grace all the more remarkable.

Harry took an instant disliking to this big, blustering braggart of a man, and pondered to what extent Lambert Ross's pompous Englishness would go. How far did he take his monetary power? To what political and business extremes did his influence reach.

There were no police or security personnel to hold back the placard wielding local objectors, which showed braveness on Lambert Ross's part but, Harry realised, this might also be a little foolhardy. He had witnessed contrived situations which were staged for maximum benefit, but these objectors seemed genuinely passionate. If trouble arose, it could mean real injury to real people.

Lambert Ross shook hands, posed for photographs, battered aside a few minor probing questions until the people followed him into Bramfield Village Hall like a flock of sheep.

Harry and Begona exchanged a glance which required no interpretation when taking two seats at the rear.

There was no microphone because Lambert Ross didn't require one. Not only was he well practised projecting his voice the stentorian boom ensured every word reached all four corners of the Village Hall. His followers and the media lapped up every one of them.

To Harry's mind, this triumph was like witnessing a great dictator reborn.

"I am humbled that you have all turned out for me today," began Lambert Ross's speech, confident that he had the room in the very palm of his hands. "I thank you all for the support you have shown me at this most difficult time. The devastating death of my son Winston has prompted me to act swiftly, more swiftly than I had planned." His pauses were precisely timed for maximum effect. "Suicide has become a tragic blight in our country. The statistics show the number of deaths per day have increased unacceptably. The yearly average has risen by five percent consistently since the pandemic. What does this say about our society? How does this reflect the culture which the Government precludes from debating? You, the people of this nation once called Great Britain, are those affected the most. These stresses which you face on a daily basis are the reason why people of all ages, sexes and races, opt to take their own life.

"They call it the cost of living crisis, blaming extraneous circumstances rather than acknowledging their own failures. Like they came up with watchwords and catchphrases for use during the Pandemic, they continue to take more time with phrases and arguments than action. You face increased prices on a daily basis! You face vast disparity amongst the haves and have nots! You look on in utter bewilderment as your elected Government let immigration soar to unsustainable levels, which puts pressure on every sector of society. And they do nothing!

"My son simply could not take this any more. He became mad as hell against this country and railed against it by tragically taking his own life, because he couldn't shoulder the burden of living any longer! How many more people will suffer? How many have already taken their lives because your Government has failed its citizens? How many will be you!

"I and my son Winston had very strained relations, there's no denying this fact. He preferred to be called Alfie, the name his mother, my devoted and darling wife, gave him. Trivia! I see that now. But I wanted my son to be proud of his name, proud of his country and his breeding. But Winston was a headstrong lad who turned into an accomplished and headstrong man. His achievements and successes are unsung. He wanted it that way."

Lambert Ross shook his head mournfully, a wistful expression of regret - well acted, thought Harry - which created a silence in the hall, even from the cynical press.

"I wish I had understood Winston more. I wish I had been a receptive listener. But I wasn't, and that's one of my failings. Nobody is perfect. I've made plenty of mistakes in my life, but this…neglect of my son, my family, is by far the worst mistake I have ever made. And that's saying something."

This caused a ripple of laughter through the auditorium. Even those who might object to this blustering, bigheaded braggart of a man were held rapt. He was humbling himself before his audience, prepping them for the big announcement, moistening them with his seductive words of redemption.

While observing every minute nuance of Lambert Ross, absorbing the words of propaganda, Harry's thoughts of doom wound their way through his brain. Was the family relationship as strained as Lambert made out? Was it a coincidence that his son attended a seminar which he had founded? The Sanctity of Sundays. Had the man on the podium instructed his son to implement the viral attack which Marti Baines unleashed yesterday, or was the son acting alone?

Lambert Ross continued, "It is with a heavy heart that today I am officially declaring my return into politics. I wish it were founded on better terms because this has been something which I have been considering for many months. I have been contemplating the state of my country, champing at the bit for the reforms which fail to appear. Tragedy has forced my hand and I can no longer stand impotently on the sidelines watching failure after failure.

"The current zeitgeist has made me feel strongly for my countrymen. Your hardships bring me frustration. Citizens of my country must not forget their past and present sacrifices. Your perennial suffering has been forced upon you by the current government, and this needs to stop at once! You should be permitted to live and not merely exist for the betterment of the self-entitled.

"I shall endeavour to be the best me I can be, as we all can hope for, and I shall be nobody's puppet. I shall not bend to convention or be broken in spirit. Our British Empire used to be a force for good but societal ennui has set in. It drains our great nation, our great English people. We need restoration and reform to bring forth our national pride once more. I anticipate pushback because that's what progress encourages. It is inevitable some people will not see the same things as I, or you, but I have and must evolve with change like we all must evolve with change, however painful that change often is. Those objectors and their opinions will wage war against me using my own past shortcomings as propaganda bait. I welcome all their opinions because life should be about diversity, not secularism. They might let slip their dogs into my path but I shall not be deterred them."

A round of applause exploded inside the small room. Even his detractors seemed to warm to Lambert's openness.

"At this early stage I cannot say which policies I will be implementing but I've certainly not been resting on my laurels these past few years in the political wilderness, be assured of that! I have monitored and studied the false promises and failed attempts of the present administration. I cannot promise there won't be any failures, but I assure you that the successes will be far greater. I cannot promise swift results, but I can promise a determined outcome. My only agenda is that I intend to invoke our national pride, while restoring our country to a glorious Great Britain once more, and a country to take pride in, and be proud of."

When he had finished, Lambert Ross fielded a few questions from the professional journalists, dishing out counter arguments with which Harry believed was, in his experience, expert public relations sophistry. He wondered how many people could see beyond the political BS. Lambert was very convincing, but he could afford the best people to create the verbal legerdemain to make him convincing. He could afford the team of people which had improved his acting skills.

# CHAPTER TWENTY-ONE

When the Q&A had finished the people followed Lambert Ross, some patting him on the shoulder, before they dispersed without further fanfare or incident. It seemed as though he had converted a faithful flock of sheep to whatever dip he had in mind for them. To Harry the lack of trouble seemed a bit of a minor miracle considering the earlier touch-paper mentality. But nothing came of the badgering and everyone went their separate ways quite amicably after Lambert Ross departed.

Harry and Begona reconvened in the car park of the Red Stag Inn after she had a few parting words to her oblique colleagues.

"Are you going straight home to Norfolk?" Begona asked.

"No. I thought I might get a ploughman's lunch here." Harry told her, meaning at the Inn. "Care to join me?"

"No can do, unfortunately. I've got a deadline to meet with this powder-keg story and I need to be back in the capital by four o'clock. This is pretty hot stuff, Harry."

"Well, no worries, and thanks for including me in this circus."

"You're welcome, Harry. Probably hear from you soon, right?"

"Most assuredly so if I find out anything juicy."

"Likewise."

Begona was on her smartphone before she was in the car. Harry gave a quick wave before he entered the Inn through its side door. The sights, smells and sounds were like any similar establishment anywhere in the country - long gone was the stale smell of tobacco. The ceiling was high with black wooden cross-beams, the walls were white-washed and decorated with local touches and flavours, the furnishings were dark wood with a little bit of the owners flamboyance, but otherwise the place was as familiar as one might expect.

One person was serving behind the bar. Six people were standing ordering or were with drinks, while half a dozen tables were already occupied. If nothing else, Lambert Ross had brought in customers for the day.

Harry ordered a large coffee, orange juice and the Ploughman's Special Lunch, as stated by the menu, although he couldn't see anything in the food listing which made it special by comparison to a regular ploughman's lunch. The friendly barman told him it might be a bit longer than usual owing to how much busier than normal it was that afternoon. Unsurprised, Harry found a twin-seated window table and glanced briefly, and disinterestedly, outside.

His mind went back to the conversation with Begona, and his reason for being here. Had he learned anything about Lambert Ross by seeing him in the flesh? Yes, was his immediate answer. Harry knew that he disliked the father more than he had disliked the son, and that was some admittance. Although Lambert hadn't shown any of the bigotry which Begona had mentioned, at least not in front of the media, where he inarguably wanted to paint the picture of a new man, grief stricken by his loss. Lambert was obviously angered at the injustices which forced his son to take his life, and his pledge that he would commit to addressing mental health issues when he returned to government rang true. The man had oozed a well coordinated and finely tuned fakery to his words, the arrogance seeping from his very pores.

Basically, Lambert Wilson was a typical politician with an agenda.

Harry certainly wouldn't put it past the man to have engineered the plot for which his son had supposedly killed himself. Although those notions were at this point merely conjecture, an undefined sixth sense.

There had been no doubting the sincerity of Winston's cleaner friend's fanatical conviction in the act she had carried out. Harry had already established that she had been genuinely distraught at Winston's death, which had been enough for her to spill the beans. Marti Baines was unfortunately a naive pawn in a bigger game and was paying the price for her trust.

Hopefully it wasn't too late to control the virus.

But was it too late to contain Lambert Ross?

When his food and drink eventually arrived after a twenty minute wait, Harry ate, drank and eavesdropped.

Several of the reporters had come in after him and they were asking the locals a few questions. The responses were often heatedly made, after the fact. They pointed retrospectively to indicate the pomposity of Ross, and several of the events carried out at Richton Hall which had prompted activists to protest them. Fox hunting had been high on their agenda, apparently. Many locals most certainly were not fans of the annual English Celebration which took place over four summer days and nights in Richton Village and on the Hall grounds, that saw general disruption and rowdiness from those who attended.

There was much bad feeling from Bramfield locals, and some extreme opinions offered. There was an understandable clash but one which make Harry like Lambert Ross less and less on each retelling.

Harry finished his lunch, thanked the barman, and went to his car. He despised procrastination so decided where his next destination would be, and what he would do when he got there.

Richton Village's ostentatious ornate wooden and wrought iron signage had recently been renovated, and it promised visitors a pleasant and quiet old English environment. The flag of St. George was a garish red slash of lines amongst the more austere characters. Harry Kovac wondered with an amused wryness how quiet the village would be on the long weekend when the English Celebration days took place, particularly the raucous Maypole festival, the traditional and modern English bands, the Morris dancing - the very thought of which forced a disdainful shudder from Harry - and the jousting tournament for all ages.

The half-mile drive through a tree lined single-lane road gave Harry the opportunity to glance at the Hall itself. From a distance he could see the private road, with its secured gate and solid wooden guard post, wound its way between well tended hedgerows and brightly coloured flower beds. An impressive wrought iron fence ran along the perimeter, disappearing amongst the wooded areas to the north and and south of the Hall as far as the eye could see, securing the grounds. The fence must be ten-feet high and was spiked at the top, an interweave of vicious razor wire glinting in the sunshine atop the entire length. Harry wondered if it was also electrified. Nothing like overkill.

The smooth surfaced village road once he passed by the Welcome To Our Village sign was just half a mile long, ending at an ancient and ornate brick entrance gate. This eighteenth century construction was the public right of way for visitors on foot to the grounds of Richton Hall.

Bold signage indicated for all vehicles to follow a gravel slip road around the back to the the car park, which was precisely what Harry did. He easily found a space and parked up. The car park could hold one-hundred vehicles and was almost full. It was obvious that Richton Village was a popular destination for day visitors during the summer - parents dragging their unwilling children around on the pretext this was a culturally significant place.

The car park was pay and display so Harry purchased a two-hour ticket.

As far as Harry could tell when he stepped onto the village road via an alleyway between early twentieth century red brick buildings, the main features here were its olde world aspect and the Hall grounds themselves. The properties were very well presented, no modern technology on show, and the eighteenth century church would certainly offer an idyllic wedding location.

There were a handful of shops selling high-priced non-souvenir boutique items, while the cafe offered homemade and home cooked food. Undoubtedly this was a popular destination for an older, maybe classier, visitor. It offered a peaceful getaway from London and its environs without being too far to travel. There was nothing Harry could see which catered for the young and more adventurous people.

Harry walked in the direction of the high walled gateway which permitted pedestrian access to the Hall ground. It was an impressive structure, ancient like the church itself and probably built around the same time, Harry guessed. It stretched about sixty yards left and right until the fence took over from its crumbling ruins. Time had eroded the remainder, with the occasional pile of rocks the only visible memory of it past glory. There were three gates of varying sizes set in arched recesses. All but one of which was closed.

There were several people milling around, either in groups or pairs. Most had their phones out, taking pictures and videos for posterity, while a couple actually had a camera which was a very rare sight these days.

The eighteenth century architecture definitely held a fascination.

When Harry and Parisa had visited Domme, in France, not three days ago there had been minimal signs of modernisation, especially in the store fronts and the restaurant, but the utter embracing of its original design underscored Richton Village's unique appeal to a more mature, cultured generation of visitor, which were definitely in the vast majority.

Harry walked along unhurriedly, trying his best to blend in but aware that would never happen. He listened and observed, noticing a few of the people who were evidently local. They were very standoffish in the most part, which was fairly understandable. Those who probably didn't take part in the festivities or didn't necessarily welcome or benefit from tourists, who lived in the village and worked elsewhere or in their homes, were probably selected by Lambert Ross for their elitist outlook. These people would evidently look down their noses at these people they assumed were the riffraff, lower or middle classes, disdainfully.

One man in country browns, greens and teals, who was an employee of Lambert Ross judging by his wheelbarrow, garden tools and the pin-badge on his lapel, was equally observant of Harry as he was himself. The man's eyes followed Harry as inconspicuously as possible while he tended the pathway flower beds, sizing him up, maybe able to recognise a man like himself, an ex-police officer, because everything about the gardener screamed ex-law enforcement to Harry. The gardener's posture, his build, the way his focus was constantly flitting around the surroundings, and his altogether alertness. Basically, the kind of person who Harry was seeking to speak with. He was throwing caution to the wind but it wasn't as if he had anything to lose, so approached the man with a plan set forth.

"Good afternoon." Harry greeted him amiably. "Are all of Lambert Ross's employee's ex-police force?"

"Most of us, sir." The gardener replied curtly, returning the amiable smile, his voice clipped English and totally unfazed by the question. "Are you looking for a job?"

"Not at the moment, no. In fact I'm on one right now. I'm a private investigator."

"And what are you investigating?"

"The death of Lambert Ross's son."

"Aren't the real police investigating his suicide?" The gardener asked without mockery, still smiling amiably, his eyes not giving anything away, if there was anything at all to give away.

"They are." Harry said. "But I'm working for a client who doesn't think it was a suicide, especially since the police have discovered Winston sabotaged the car of my colleague two days prior."

"Interesting. Good luck. I'm sorry that I can't be of help."

"No problem. Thanks for listening."

Harry walked away, smiling to himself. He had had enough of this air of gentrification and hoped prodding the hornets nest would succeed in putting the cat amongst the pigeon's. If not, if he was considered nothing more than small fry, Harry had lost nothing.

He pulled out his smartphone and single-touched to call Parisa's phone. She answered almost immediately.

"Hi, darling."

"Hi." Harry responded.

"Are you home soon? I came back early because I'm missing you."

"And I'm missing you, too," Harry grinned; obviously Parisa's work in Scotland had concluded earlier than anticipated, "but I'm afraid not. Can you tell Daphne that I'm staying here at Richton tonight, and to forward anything by email that I might need to know."

"Okay." Parisa sounded disappointed. "Are you onto something?"

"Probably nothing, but I'm hoping to meet Lambert Ross sometime, possibly tonight, but most likely tomorrow."

"Okay. Love you." Parisa did not need to remind Harry to be careful, so she didn't waste the words.

"I'll call you later. Love you."

Harry disconnected the call.

# CHAPTER TWENTY-TWO

The Red Stag Inn had half a dozen medium-sized rooms, and two family sized. One of each was available for Harry's consideration. He was grateful they had any availability at all although he had noted earlier the midweek trade might preclude a lack of bed and breakfast customers, also he wasn't overly fussy, so Harry chose the medium one.

He had no luggage so brought no ablutions with him. He ambled up High Street to the village convenience store and purchased a toothbrush, toothpaste and deodorant, paying more than he normally would but he wasn't overly bothered by the extra expense.

Harry's room at the Red Stag Inn was located in an annex block behind the car park with a glass corridor linking the two buildings. It was a room shaped room with standard unfussy furniture. The bathroom was what might be described as functional without space to swing the proverbial cat. All told, it suited Harry's requirements and nothing more.

Harry undressed, showered and sat upon the springy bed mattress, opening the email app on his phone and reading and replying to those messages which he deemed more important, while binning the junk. He sent a message to Parisa which described the room and ended with a laughing emoji.

He dressed and left the grounds of the Inn, walking along Main Street for the fresh air and to be seen. Harry was a newcomer. Maybe someone who had been at the Lambert Ross event would recognise him as being an attendee, maybe not. Maybe someone working for Ross would report back that he was still in the Village, maybe not. His hope was, after telling the Richton Village gardener what his purpose was, that the news of a Private Investigator in the vicinity and that a probable murder investigation was being carried by the Norfolk CID, would be reported back to the boss. Harry's background would undoubtedly be checked by Lambert Ross's own people, and one of the wannabe politicians lackeys might turn up here and ask a few questions personally.

A long shot for sure, but one worth attempting after putting the cat amongst the pigeons.

If nothing and nobody turned up tonight, then Harry would just have to pay Lambert's fiefdom another visit tomorrow and rattle the cage a little less discretely than he had earlier.

After fresh air and a walk had achieved nothing, Harry returned to the Red Stag Inn where he ordered a bottle of Merlot to have with cottage pie and seasonal vegetables - nobody would be aware that alcohol had absolutely no effect on his metabolism.

It was happy hour so there were a dozen patrons.

"There was a lot of hatred toward Lambert Ross from the villagers here earlier." Harry said to the barman, who turned out to be the owner of the establishment. He said this in a loud enough voice so the other patrons within earshot couldn't fail to hear. "I'm wondering what initially provoked it. Surely he must be good for local trade?"

"Doesn't help us, any." The owner offered indifferently. "Are you a reporter?"

"Oh, no. I'm a private investigator." Harry said without elaborating. "I came along with a friend who is a journalist and thought I'd snoop around. I'm a naturally inquisitive guy."

"Ross is a racist bigot." One of the barflies piped up, pint in hand.

"And sexist." Offered his female companion without need of interpretation, it was clear she despised the man.

Harry nodded. "I had certainly gathered the man's personality is slightly misaligned and like all politicians he is good with the vitriolic rhetoric, but what are his people like? Do they fully ascribe to his beliefs?"

"Definitely." Said the barfly without hesitation.

"Only his employees." The owner offered defensively. "The people who live in his village, the residents, we don't see them a great deal."

"Privileged rich white men!" Said the woman disgustedly. "All of them. I'm not fooling."

"Racist and sexist." The barfly said. "Like we said."

There was a mumble of assent from a few others.

"Money talks to money." The owner said, not unreasonably because that was an unarguable truism. "A few of the people passing through here on their way back from Ross's village stop by, but very rarely do we see any of his own guys, and definitely none of the village residents. Unless there's some event like today."

"Do you think Ross has a hope?" Harry asked the bar. "I mean, getting back into politics."

The woman snorted derisively.

"Probably." Said the barfly wearily. "Lets face facts shall we: how many people actually remember what he did all those years ago; how many real people actually know what he does in his own home? Too few make any real impact on us. Some reporter or whatever, no disrespect, drags up old stories. So what? People like a redemption story. Ross is so full of the same BS as all politicians that the uninformed mind can't see through the deception."

All the patrons seemed to be in agreement, raising their glasses to toast the fact.

Harry thought the observation was astute. He told the owner: "With those sentiments, I'll pay for the next round."

Murmurs of thanks greeted Harry as he took his glass and bottle of wine to a seat by the window which offered a view of the Village Hall apex road. The heated political conversation at the bar continued unabated, with Harry overhearing partial words.

While contemplating the evening a figure sashayed into his periphery. Harry looked up. A woman stood there. She was in her late twenties, dressed in a nurses uniform with added jacket and non-work shoes. She had obviously finished her day shift because she held a half-consumed pint glass of beer and her cheeks were red, signifying that she was in no state to drive anywhere to a job at the nearest hospital, which Harry knew from his research was fifteen miles away. He had noticed her earlier sitting alone in a cubicle back of the bar.

"May I...?" She indicated the seat opposite him. "I'll be quick. I'll leave when your meal arrives."

Harry remembered her from the Lambert Ross event. Then, she had been an objector to the politician, angry but silent, seething emotions roiling over her. Harry was naturally curious to hear what she had to say, so he beckoned for her to join him.

"I'm Rosita." She formally introduced herself. She was slightly drunk, and shook his hand too firmly. "My husband-" her eyes immediately filled with tears and she looked away, angered and embarrassed by the display. "God, I'm sorry." She wiped the tears away, breathed in, composed herself. "It's only been six months. Sorry.

Strewth, I'm a mess. Anyway, let me… My husband was a reporter. He worked in London, we lived here. I still do. He was researching something on Lambert Ross, something he thought was important before… Before Lambert Ross killed him."

Harry raised a quizzical eyebrow.

"Or, not Ross, but he had someone do it." She finished.

Harry was about to ask a question but she raised a hand to silence him while trying her best to maintain composure. Harry watched as this poor woman, evidently still mourning the death of her husband, wrung emotional wounds from her face.

"I went to the police," Rosita continued, "but they said my husband had been in an accident. There was nothing suspicious about. So they said. And that was that but I know there was much more."

"I see." Was all Harry could offer because as soon as his meal arrived she left the table, apologising for having disturbed him, shoulders slumped dejectedly.

The owner set the steaming plate of cottage pie with green and orange seasonal vegetables on the table, with napkin-wrapped fork and knife. When Rosita was out of earshot, the owner said in a soft voice: "Poor Rosita. I presume she told you about her husband. She is positive he was murdered but…she is still clutching at straws." He shrugged sympathetically. "Anyway, enjoy your food."

"Thank you."

The food was undeniably excellent. The cottage pie was homemade, the vegetables fresh and the gravy was rich and tasty. While eating, Harry's thoughts were scatter-shod. Foremost he was giving consideration to what the nurse had told him, yet unfortunately the cynical side of his mind reasoned that she was emotionally exhausted because of the loss she had suffered and, like the owner of the Red Stag Inn had told him, Rosita was clutching at straws. It was a common enough story. Losing a loved one made people reactionary, forcing emotions to become extreme and unclear. Time was indeed the greatest healer.

Time had certainly healed the rift between Lambert Ross and his estranged son, Winston Alfred, to the point of a secretive alliance between them, if that had indeed been the case. Harry wondered where the son had hoped this renewed relationship would lead. Harry wouldn't put it past a man like Lambert to orchestrate events for purely political reasons and, at the end, to disown and discredit his son. Which would have been risky, considering. Now, of course, that had become a moot point. Winston had committed suicide. Or at least that's what the public assumed. DCI Gnanakaran had indeed inferred there was cause to believe foul play rather than suicide had been the cause of Winston Ross's demise.

Had Lambert Ross, as one of that days reporters jokingly inferred, actually orchestrated the murder of his son? That would certainly cover up any link between their actions. How would the politician react to the police investigation regarding the sabotage of Zero's car by his son?

Clutching at straws seemed to be a running theme, Harry thought ruefully.

The Red Stag Inn had now gotten busier. A half dozen people asking for food, but mostly they were social drinkers. Harry had casually observed all the patrons coming and going. One woman had caught his attention more than the other people, although she had done her best to blend in. She was a professional. Another ex-police service member in the employ of Lambert Ross, no doubt. Of this, Harry was certain. Standing at the bar she ordered an orange juice, trying her best to remain aloof without attracting attention to herself, and failing miserably. She was another stranger to the Red Stag Inn like Harry, which didn't take a detective to work out!

Once Harry had finished his food the owner cleared the table.

"Would you like dessert?" He asked. "Today's special is a delicious rhubarb crumble and custard. My husband made it this afternoon."

"Lovely. Yes please."

Harry was briefly on his own again. He looked out the window but sensed movement in his direction, before he saw the woman in Ross's employ. Harry didn't look up when he addressed her.

"Please, sit." He offered.

The woman lowered herself into the chair opposite, watching him cautiously, curiously.

"Police or military?" Harry asked casually, turning to face her, looking her in the eyes with the intimidating dead-eyed expression perfected over years in law enforcement.

"Both." She replied. "I was military police."

"I'm impressed. I presume your orders are to assess me before approaching me?" Harry said. "Well, what's your verdict?"

She was in her mid-thirties, so far as Harry could surmise. Her blonde hair had been cropped short while in the service, but was now longer and tied and swept back from her short fringe. She had piercingly blue eyes, unnaturally so, which made Harry think she was wearing contacts. Maybe poor eyesight was why she left the service? Her cheek bones were high and she smiled easily between thin unpainted lips. No doubt she kept herself in shape and would be a fast, formidable opponent.

"You were a good police officer, once." She told Harry emotionlessly. "Now you're a private investigator, and a good one, apparently, at least according to the press. If push comes to shove you can no doubt handle yourself, that's for sure but that would be a last resort."

"You obviously didn't read all that from looking at me." Harry observed with a chuckle.

"No. I'm Mister Ross's chief of security and as you are well aware the internet is one of our tools."

"I didn't realise Lambert Ross employed women, let alone one as his security chief." Harry stated, which was true, especially from what he had heard that very evening. "He seems very traditional, sexist, even."

"Times change. Mister Ross made an exception." She offered.

"And he no doubt needs to give the outward impression of a changed man. Progressive in the eyes of the public. He was wise sending you. An unfamiliar man in here might've aroused local suspicions, especially as their backs are up after his self-aggrandising speech earlier today. A woman projects less force."

"You're not local yourself. How are these people treating you."

"I'm not. But then I told these nice people who I am right off the bat, told them exactly why I am here, too."

"And why are you here, Mister Kovac?"

"I'm here to ruffle a few feathers, so to speak. Put the cat amongst the pigeons. But more to the point, what does Lambert Ross have to say to me? I presume you're his messenger."

She nodded with a wry smile, "Mister Ross wonders if you are available for luncheon tomorrow?"

Harry nodded and tried not to look too pleased with this reaction to his presence from Lambert Ross. "Sounds fine. His place or mine?"

"Richton Hall, naturally."

"Naturally."

Lambert Ross's messenger raised herself from the chair, not removing her eyes from his, "Be careful, Mister Kovac."

"Take care of me personally, will you."

"If needs must."

"What are you afraid of?" Harry asked.

"Nothing." Came the blunt reply.

# CHAPTER TWENTY-THREE

Next morning after showering and dressing Harry called Parisa to update her on his plans for the day, his invite to Lambert Ross's fiefdom, and also to check his messages which, as per usual, were plentiful, some good, some immediately junked.

DCI Gnanakaran showered him with myriad nuggets of information, for which Harry would be eternally grateful; they had discovered no directly incriminating link between Lambert Ross regarding his sons actions. After examining Zero's car thoroughly it had been found that foul play was indeed involved; extraneous details were omitted by DCI Gnanakaran, to save Harry time. Marti Baines had utterly confessed her guilt and had told them everything Winston Ross had instructed her to carry out surrounding the chemical attack. Investigators were furiously wracking their resources to discover the exact compounds involved. The media have been informed, instructed to maintain some semblance of calm to their reportage at this early stage.

Harry wondered how Lambert Ross would react to this new situation attributable to his son.

Lastly, Teri Hamilton filled him in regarding the DB5 hunt, telling him their offices had been ransacked by persons unknown - speculating that it was most likely linked to the gentleman who Harry met two days ago. Smith and Climmy's increased payment and insistence they carry on their investigation despite the threats, offered proof that Harry had been right when assessing they would not be put off by any threats. JP had been in contact from France with a possible connection for Adam Richardson, which Teri was presently investigating.

Harry didn't know what the firm would've done without Teri's assistance at this present time. Not only had she started her employment earlier than initially intended, but she had stepped seamlessly into the role.

With time on his hands, Harry had an unhurried breakfast at the Red Stag Inn and read one of the many complimentary newspapers, choosing The Daily Telegraph for no particular reason, because essentially he believed they all printed biased propaganda articles solely to sell their own brand.

Their inevitable front page story was about Lambert Ross's announcement of yesterday and the many and varied reactions surrounding it, with the byline 'Lambert Ross Cries Havoc.' After a few select phrases quoted from his speech there followed a mixture of opinion, swinging from positive to negative and those who couldn't care less. A quote was attributed directly to the Prime Minister: "I wish Mister Lambert Ross sincere condolences on his most profound loss and the best of luck in his political endeavours going forward." Which was an innocuous sound bite anyone or AI could have written, and probably had done so.

There was no mention in the newspaper about Winston Alfred Ross's illegal activities. Those allegations would undoubtedly be abundantly evident in the hyperbolic tabloids. It was an easy deduction for Harry to conclude that somebody's paymaster would keep inflammatory statements about a client out of the respected newspapers, for now at least. Money and influence talked in this world, that was a commonly known given, and Lambert Ross had ample funds of both at his disposal.

The more Harry was learning about Lambert Ross's past, his nationalistic views and ancient prejudices, plus the great lengths he had gone to when it came to covering up historic family transgressions, the more certain Harry became that the actions of his son Winston were interlinked.

Harry set off from the Red Stag Inn at eleven o'clock, arriving at the half-full Pay and Display car park in Richton Village and purchasing a half-day ticket. Better to be safe than sorry.

Today must generally be a quieter day because there were fewer tourists, unless yesterday was busy simply because of the announcement in the next village. Maybe lunchtime was busier. There were only two people by the church. These were the only ones Harry saw until he went through the gate which gained pedestrian access to the grounds of Richton Hall.

The estate was vast, stretching out in all directions. It not only encompassed the village, but also a great swathe of beautifully tended gardens either side of the curving driveway, marked with evenly spaced oak trees. A lake which was just about visible as the land dropped off to the northern boundary of the lawn glistened in the sunlight, while sprawling woodland bordered the entire expanse.

With the summer sunshine blazing upon the myriad flowers and trees Harry could appreciate the appeal to visitors and locals alike. If nothing else, Lambert Ross was lucky to enjoy such splendour on a daily basis. This was a fiefdom of which one could take great pride and pleasure.

Harry walked unhurriedly, drinking in the splendour. He still had plenty of time to absorb his surroundings, not that he anticipated trouble, but in his profession one cannot he too cautious.

An estate gardener, different to the fellow who Harry spoke to yesterday, riding an electric single-seat vehicle drove by him and nodded amiably.

Harry caught sight of Richton Hall when he rounded the sweeping driveway, the main building and its various annexes still some four-hundreds distant.

The Hall was the dominant building and if not for the blazing overhead sunlight it would look quite bleak and foreboding. With its greys and dark red brick construction there was an unloved quality to it. The dark framed windows and red-tile roof were embellished with auspicious finials, buttresses and parapets. Certainly there was nothing resplendent about the severe oblong, three-storey construction.

What the original designer had intended was most profoundly lost on Harry, and he filed that question away for later.

Thankfully the Hall was saved by the two less imposing outbuildings which thrust forward from its sides resplendently. One was a pink-clad, glass domed studio, with flamboyant modern art painted on its inward facing wall. Opposite this was the original glass-house apiary which had a dividing central partition to keep the conservatory living space separate from the original intended use, where over-sized plants existed within plus what, to Harry's eyes, looked like grape vines.

The courtyard joined the driveway and access road, which disappeared amongst trees, and had an overly elaborate yet bizarrely austere fountain as its centrepiece with a flag pole proudly displaying a gently fluttering flag of St. George.

Harry was no judge of architectural design but this was certainly doing nothing for him!

The right-hand of the two imposing front entrance doors opened and a man exited. He was studious of face, perhaps in his late sixties, and sported the attire one might associate with a traditional English butler. Formality was certainly at the forefront of Lambert's Ross's philosophy, on the surface, at least. Harry wondered if the extent of that tradition included the more barbarous aspects of English history. If Richton Hall itself was anything to go by then that was a distinct possibility.

"Good morning, Mister Kovac." The butler's words consisted of precisely formed vowels, consonants and syllables. When Harry shook his hand, the grip was firm and dry. "My name is Gough, sir. I am the estate manager and butler. The Master has been detained but luncheon should commence in about thirty minutes. I hope that is acceptable?"

"Yes, thank you." Harry responded to what was a rhetorical question because he had no real say in the matter.

"Very good, sir. Would you care for a tour of the Hall?"

"By all means, Gough, that sounds marvellous."

"First of all, sir." Gough held out the silver tray which he had held all this time. "If you don't mind leaving your mobile phone with me, sir. For security reasons, you understand."

"Of course." Harry reluctantly handed over his telephone. Did the politician not want his conversations recorded?

They passed through a small lobby into the main hallway where ancient wooden benches faced each other, a sweeping scroll of Olde English etched deeply into their seats. The high ceiling featured a ornately carved fox hunting scene, three-storeys up, the colours faded over two-centuries. The broad circular ground floor ended at the staircase which zigzagged upward, two landings extending onto either floor with their balconies embracing each other above the lobby like pincers of a crab, forming perfect perimeter circles.

Gough performed his role as tour guide with knowledgeable aplomb and obvious pride - he clearly shared his bosses national pride, not that there was anything wrong with it, so long as that pride didn't turn into fanaticism. Gough showed Harry all the public facing rooms with their many British antiques and features which no doubt appealed to history buffs. Apparently many had been recovered from the great corners of the global Empire which Britannia once oversaw before dissolution.

Harry noted the family portraits which were hung either side of the central corridor were male dominated. The poses were of straight backed, formally attired, stern and fussy gentlemen and, at least in Harry's mind, self-aggrandising pomposity through the ages.

Hardly surprising to any visitor, least of all Harry, but the rooms had definite English blandishments, taking pride in national historic events and sites with many paintings depicting significant achievements and successes. Flags were aloft. Not all of the images in the paintings were tasteful to a modern eye. One showed fox hunting where the animal had clearly been caught and was being torn apart, while another proudly depicted an English trade ship whose Captain was meting out punishment to a colonial captive. Lambert Ross undoubtedly defended their importance so they stayed where they were.

Royalty was well represented in portraits and personal photographs with them, but not in an extensively obsessional way, just enough of an homage for that esteemed family, respectful without being subjugating.

The tour, presumably the same which was given to paying visitors, covered about a third of the Hall's floor space and lasted for exactly thirty minutes. Harry wondered if his lordship had deliberately chosen the delay to show off these very nationalist trappings from an Empire long gone. He certainly wouldn't put it past the man.

"Thank you, Gough." Harry offered once it became clear the tour had ended. "It was very enlightening."

"You are welcome, sir." Gough bowed gratefully.

Now, Harry thought, it was into the dragons lair.

## CHAPTER TWENTY-FOUR

The octagonal conservatory table had six seats arranged around it all bearing a unique repurposed aesthetic, and were positioned in the shaded quarter of the large glass enclosure. Solar-powered fans cooled the air. Place settings were for the two occupants of the table, Harry Kovac and Lambert Ross. Gough brought before them a tower of cucumber finger sandwiches, a cake stand with a variety of sweet pastries, on a silver serving tray with matching silver teapot, cafeteria containing pitch black coffee, Wedgwood fine china sugar pot and milk pourer, plus cups, saucers, plates and cutlery.

Lambert Ross had a silver cigar box and cube shaped lighter on his side of the table. Both objects bore intricate detailing of a countryside scenic nature, with a flag of St. George being carried by a knight, and were clearly old. Possibly a cherished family heirloom which, considering the general view of smokers and smoking, exhibited a robust rebellious streak to the man.

The tea party lunch was very formal and, in Harry's estimation, a fussy display of pompous Englishness.

"Thank you, Gough." Lambert spoke in clipped, precise, English which sounded forced, much like that of the well practiced butler. Harry wondered if ever the accent slipped, maybe when the man became excited and forgot his airs and graces, or perhaps when he was drunk on his sherry!

Gough silently withdrew from the conservatory.

"You enjoyed Gough's tour, Mister Kovac?" Lambert stated rather than asked, leaning forward in his seat with expectant interest.

"Yes, thank you, it was quite illuminating. Your butler told me that your family entrusted the design with the eighteenth century anti-establishment zealot Jason Oxer. I'm no expert on the subject but wasn't that considered a bit controversial at the time?"

Lambert Ross's eyes seemed to light up with excitement and he gave a tilt of the head to acknowledge Harry's keen observation. All seemed perfectly amicable between them at the moment but Harry knew he was the fly being led into a spiders web by this man.

"It certainly was against the social and political grain at the time." Lambert agreed. "And my ancestors did keep journals, but alas, there is no mention of motive for their decision to use Oxer. My family have always been staunch believers in the tradition of the English constitution which does make their choice a curious one indeed." He acknowledged. "I have unsuccessfully endeavoured to trace their motives to the utmost of my powers," Lambert poured himself some tea, not offering to do the same for Harry, "Which are considerable. I'm sure they did what they thought at the time to be appropriate, yet this Hall itself is sadly testament to their often bad judgement." He harrumphed, which seemed to be his way of laughing. "If not for its historical significance and protected status I confess I would have the ancient pile razed, with a more appropriate and tasteful construction erected in its place."

"Something with more pompous grandeur, perhaps?"

Lambert Ross laughed.

Harry poured himself some of the hot coffee from the cafeteria into a delicate Wedgwood cup, aware that Ross's eyes bored into the top of his skull. Was this staunchly English man going to rile easily? When was the true nature of this invitation going reveal itself?

The coffee smelled divine and Harry wished the cup was bigger, but that would be anathema to the moment. He plopped in a sugar cube and stirred the contents with deliberate delicately, using one of the silver spoons, thinking when in England one should act as the English aristocracy do.

Lambert Ross pulled a cigar from the box. It was about six-inches in length and possessed an impressive girth. Was the man compensating. He offered one to Harry, who declined.

"They are produced here," Ross said, "in England. I own the sole farm in Tenterton which does so. They produce wine and champagne for me also, which I stock in the cellar. None of that foreign muck for me." He sighed. "You know, my Elizabeth would have transformed this place," Ross stated, subject changed, genuinely rueful for the loss of his wife, "if she had been afforded longer on this earth to have the opportunity. The exterior would have been much more flamboyant and gay, like you correctly asserted. Elizabeth would have injected more pomp and grandeur to this old pile." He harrumphed. "You saw the interior rooms she was able to transform, at least those which are open to the general public. Privately, Elizabeth's wilful utilisation of colour still dazzles me despite her absence. She certainly brought much needed gaiety to my world when I needed it, that is for certain." Ross sighed heavily. "But alas, my Elizabeth is no longer with us so rumination and dreaming are quite fruitless endeavours."

The older man helped himself to one of his own plates and clumsily took three fingers of the cucumber sandwiches, muttering irritably about something or other. Lambert Ross had big hands which weren't made for delicacy. Harry was frankly surprised that he even entertained the use of fine sets of delicate bone crockery, especially if these ones were precious family heirlooms. There was obvious prestige in showing off one's wares to the plebiscite, so maybe these fragile objects only came out of their cupboards when Ross had visitors to impress. Not to mention the very blatant Englishness of it.

"So, Mister Harry Kovac. You are a private investigator?" Lambert Ross's question was bluntly directed. He knew the answer and was well aware of all the answers which Harry might offer him, but this arrogant self-important politician could at least pretend to be inclusive.

"That's right. You probably already know I retired from Scotland Yard a few years ago under amicable circumstances." Harry said the last part with the wryness which it deserved. "I moved to quiet Norfolk and joined Crane Investigation Services, which has since proven the opposite of quiet, yet by comparison to London it's mostly sedate. I became a partner last year mainly because of the success I had in Berlin."

"Yes, I heard about your much vaunted discovery of a Cold War nuclear weapon in the very heart of Germany. One can only imagine the devastation it would have wrought if it had gotten into the hands of terrorists. Well done, the world owes you a great debt of gratitude."

"Thank you."

"Your firm gained great publicity from this success, I understand?"

Harry nodded amicably, "It did indeed. Business has increased yet Norwich and the Norfolk countryside is still considered off the beaten track. I suppose that's why it's easy for criminal activities to proceed unchecked with relative anonymity."

"I agree." Ross said, his face displaying no tell-take giveaway signs to the underhand accusation Harry had just made. "My estate here feels a world away from the hustle and bustle of London and Parliament. I've grown quite accustomed to the privacy which fortitude has brought me. My Hall, my Village, my estate. It has humbled me. You heard my speech yesterday. Of course it was inevitable I should bide my time before making a triumphant return to the arena. I admit that I had planned to return all along. It was an…unforeseen tragedy which forced my hand, and despite my son distancing himself from me I am heartbroken at his passing and senseless waste of life." Lambert held up his hand to ward off anything Harry might have to say against this. "I know the truth, Mister Kovac. I know how my son died. I know what he did. Suicide is often perceived as the cowards escape from reality, but I truly believe it was the system which failed my son, as it does many other people." He leaned forward to emphasise his words. "Do you know the statistics for suicide, Mister Kovac? Of course not, why should you. Why should anyone. The present government hide the facts, bury the truth, ignore the reality of their failings. If I were to tell you that since the Pandemic there has been a five-hundred percent increase in suicides amongst English men, would that shock you?"

Harry said that yes it would, because the fact was, the increase was staggeringly awful.

"The statistics for women are lower. Half that." Ross said disdainfully. "And this is one of the numerous failures which I shall address. It's unacceptable. Do you know why there are so many suicides amongst English men? Its because there are too many immigrants coming into our country. These reprehensible freeloaders are destroying our infrastructure. Elections roll around, the political parties trot out the same claims every time, promising to reduce this, increase that. Balderdash! Propaganda for the common man. But I shall keep my promises." He gestured grandly. "You see this estate. I have money, I have power in my own kingdom. I don't need the bribes or backhanders which other politicians receive. I have made my own money, my own power. I don't need these things which others seek from politics." He harrumphed. "Yes, I'm not totally altruistic. Nobody who desires the top position does it simply because they want to make a difference to those less fortunate, and to think such would be naïve. I have a privileged position which I'm not about to exploit solely for my own personal advantage."

Lambert Ross paused. His chest was puffed up beneath his white shirt and Etonian tie. Even the blind could see how proud a man he was, how much he loved the sound of his own voice, how thoroughly he enjoyed rolling the words about and spitting them out with aplomb. Lambert Ross was undeniably charismatic but utterly lacked charm; intelligent without empathy. Like most men in power or from the establishment he lacked any sense of humility or respect for the people and the world around him. That too was evident when reading between the lines. It was not just a rumour propitiated by the locals. This man, like his son, was evidently a sexist, racist, elitist bigot.

How would Lambert Ross fair in parliament after years in the wilderness? Had the perceptions from the media altered? Would they embrace this new man? Even if the new man was surface decor only. Harry doubted Lambert really cared about the perceptions of others, he was not worried about a backlash from his son's actions or the dredging of his past.

"I do not like duplicitous people, Mister Kovac." Ross abruptly stated. His eyes locked onto Harry's, boring into the back of his skull as if trying to rip the very thoughts from Harry's mind. "So tell me. Why are you here?"

"Because I was invited."

Lambert Ross stared blankly at Harry, unmoved by the facetious humour.

"Some people use humour in the face of fear, Mister Kovac," said Ross. "What do you fear about a question so simple that my five year-old grandson could grasp?"

"In fact," said Harry, "I was invited to your meeting yesterday by a friend, a political reporter, and decided to stay on. It was merely happenstance that you should invite me here once you discovered I was a private investigator, and you obviously learnt of my other purpose here after I mentioned to your help that your son had sabotaged my partners car. Then there is the virus your son developed and unleashed. So I think it is you who are frightened. Frightened that I might discover the secret about the death of your son."

"Bah! There is no secret, Mister Kovac." Ross said with off-handed contempt. "Winston committed suicide and to be frank, any aid you can provide is invaluable. We both know the police are investigating this tragedy. Winston was guilty of developing a new COVID type virus, so I've been told, and the records will show his guilt. But I am riled by the injustice brought upon my family by the sorely lacking mental health system which drove him to it. Their own failure led to my sons fate. The system conveniently forgets about people like my son. He helped with a cure for COVID, for goodness sake! Why did nobody recognise Winston's mental health illness? Why did the people he worked with not detect his illness? It is this system you should be more concerned about, Mister Kovac. It is they to whom your investigation should be targeted.

"I have not…that is, my son Winston and I had become what the press diplomatically dubbed as estranged. We were torn asunder by life itself, I will admit to that, and it was utterly my failing. I am to blame as much as my son, maybe more so, because of my lifestyle and how I have chosen to live my life. It goes with the territory, I'm sorry to say. A man in the public eye neglects certain aspects of the world around him and in my case it was unfortunately my family. But now I've been graced with the insight to realise there is an alternative way."

"How do you account for your son attending your Sanctity of Sundays meetings?" Harry asked.

Lambert's eyes blazed with anger. "What?"

"Winston and the woman who he got to unleash the virus attended meetings of The Sanctity of Sunday." Harry stated. "Your own group of fanatics."

"Coincidence." Lambert harrumphed. "I did not know he attended these meetings, but I will blame myself for not keeping in contact with Winston. I will blame myself for this tragedy, Mister Kovac, and therefore I do not appreciate, to use a vulgar Americanism, a gumshoe, poking his nose into my business. Especially not now. I am building up my political empire and any interference from an amateur organisation is unwarranted. I have matters more important than your personal interests to be concerned with. I have much to do to rehabilitate the public perception of me. There is much rebuilding of my image to achieve but those building blocks have a foundation, a very sturdy foundation. I want this country turned around. I want justice for English citizens. And I demand justice for my son.

"If you want to help me, Mister Kovac, then so be it, but otherwise you need to know this," he leaned forward with well practiced menace. "You mean nothing to me. You are no more than a little fish swimming downstream toward an ocean full of sharks and if I choose to do so, I can bring all to bear upon you and your reputation!"

The conservatory fell deafeningly silent except for the chattering of the birds outside. The menace had seeped most strongly from the words said by Lambert Ross. Harry had no illusion about the unspoken lines between. Political sophistry at it's height. Harry was now, more than ever, convinced beyond the shadow of a doubt that Lambert Ross was in some way responsible for the death of his own son. Now all that remained was for Harry to prove it.

"Fair enough," Harry said, not at all undeterred as was the politician's aim. "But I am a resourceful man, Mister Ross, and won't stop until I find out the reason why my boss, my business partner, my friend…was killed."

Lambert Ross nodded, studying Harry thoughtfully. He sipped his tea, not taking his eyes off the man in front of him. Finally Lambert seemed to make his mind up about something which had been conflicting within his mind. He smiled a sharks smile, his eyes suddenly darkening, all emotion erased except for a certain amount of gratification.

"Come, Mister Kovac!" Lambert Ross said, visage transforming to its previously hospitable incarnation. "Let us not fall out about such things. I would like to introduce you to a part of this estate to which Gough did not show you. It's part of the rear annex which I'm particularly proud of, where I keep my most sacred trophies, ones which I know you will appreciate and maybe give you more insight into my, how shall we say it, predilections as an Englishman."

Gough arrived from the Hall doorway as if he had been summoned by some invisible force.

"Ah, Gough, nicely timed." Lambert said, rubbing his hands together with unfettered glee. "I thought we might introduce our guest to the trophy room." He harrumphed heartily at the very notion.

"As you wish, sir." Gough bowed acquiescence without hesitation, then indicated with a slight flourish of his right hand to Harry. "If you would care to follow me, sir."

Harry figured this pompous English politician wanted to show-off some hunting trophies to the plebiscite, things which were possibly distasteful to a more general audience. They would be stuffed animals and the like from a more archaic time. Lambert Ross wanted to boast about his own manliness, and intimidate, of course. A common trait of the rich and powerful, at least it was in Harry's experience, with few exceptions to the rule. Harry was too intrigued to decline, his curiosity about this man was peaked. Not that this trophy room would contain anything which might be legally awkward, so there wasn't much to gain except extra insight.

Gough led them through the main hallway and unlocked and opened a door alongside the one which led into the kitchen, where Harry had received the earlier tour. They stepped into a corridor lit by a single hanging pendant light, which had only one door leading off it about thirty feet from at the entrance.

Harry followed Gough who produced another key and unlocked this final door. Lambert Ross shut the door behind them.

They stepped into a windowless room with a light which automatically sprang to life, illuminating this new enclosure. Harry had been expecting to see the contents of a roomful of trophies, yet there were none.

Both side walls had benches running their entire length and had placed upon them tools of the taxidermy trade, with a clean white basin in their middle. The traditional tools were spotlessly clean and appeared unused. On the walls hung archaic variations of medical instruments, some which might be used for taxidermy from a more barbaric era.

"You like it, Mister Kovac?" Lambert Ross asked in a matter-of-fact voice.

"It's a bit underwhelming." Harry admitted truthfully, although he was inwardly seething because he instinctively knew what was coming next.

Gough was now holding a small-calibre revolver which was pointed at Harry.

"Are you really going to shoot me?" Harry asked, unperturbed by the gun. "And then what will you do, chop me up into little pieces to feed the dogs." Harry laughed at the pure absurdity of the idea. "Obviously you wouldn't do such a thing because too many people know I'm here, but I don't have to tell you that, it's not like you're stupid!"

"Oh no, Mister Kovac," said Lambert Ross with a satisfied chuckle. "But we will require the keys to your car first."

"Place them on the floor." Gough ordered, his manner broaching no argument. "Then take ten paces backward, if you please."

Realising the futility of resisting, Harry placed his keys on the floor before himself and stepped back as instructed. His jaw worked furiously while wondering how much of a fool he had been to be led into this trap. Truth be told, there had been no indication of this kind of danger, this extreme measure which Lambert Ross had embarked upon. If the man was capable of this, wondered Harry, what else was he capable of?

Lambert Ross scooped up the keys, grinning with boorish satisfaction.

"You are of course familiar with the short story by Richard Connell entitled The Most Dangerous Game." The brusque politician stated. "It's a tried and true story one-hundred years old, Mister Kovac, did you know that? I am also informed that it has been adapted and copied on numerous occasions throughout the years by other authors, and film makers too, so I understand, not that I watch such drivel.

"I myself was introduced to the story many years ago," the politician continued, "while with my father in our last English overseas outpost. A friend of my father's employed the game at his plantation to keep his employees in check. Unfortunately he was foolhardy and blatant with his game. The authorities in his country couldn't turn a blind eye forever so offered this man an ultimatum: leave their land or be arrested and humiliated. He chose to raze the property to the ground, killing himself and his family and employees." Lambert Ross paused briefly, eyes glowing with pride. "I adopted his game but have been far more selective in my prey. Could you imagine the scandal if this brutality were discovered to be happening in good old England?" He laughed. "The bodies of the people I choose are disposed of in such a way as to remove any trace. Their death is attributed to having occurred elsewhere, because, like your own car and phone, there will be proof that you left here alive. Tonight you shall experience this most exciting sport firsthand. Please feel free to furnish whatever rudimentary weapons you can from the objects collected within this room, to at least give yourself a fighting chance, although you truly have none, but you may consider yourself part of a very select group of people, Mister Kovac. And of course, I wish you luck."

With these final words, and before Harry could reply, Lambert Ross and his butler left him alone in the room.

## CHAPTER TWENTY-FIVE

Once the door was locked Harry nonetheless tried the handle, just in case of some oversight. There was no give in the door however much force he applied. Next he tried the handleless door at the far end with his full weight behind his shoulder, feet firmly planted for maximum pressure, but achieved nothing better than discomfort to his sinews.

Obviously the room would be soundproofed so there would be no point calling for help.

Harry Kovac realised that Lambert Ross was truly mad. Not only had this bigot plotted his return to politics after years in the wilderness, he had lost all reason during that period. The origins of this game which Lambert had conceived stretched back further than the short story by Richard Connell. Many of the early English monarchs had enjoyed the sport as a way of eliminating undesirable elements within their kingdom, and this in turn had resulted in what polite society considered to be the less barbaric practice of fox hunting. The self-imposed establishment used the reasoning that they were culling a predatory population which threatened livestock, whereas it was to satisfy their continued need to prove their power extended to the very nature of life and death.

Harry could not believe he had been so utterly stupid as to be led into a trap such as this. And yet who knew that even in this day and age of almost total surveillance a man, even one as high-profile as Lambert Ross, could get away with committing murder and covering it up so completely?

Clearly this mans success rate was one-hundred percent because no escapee would remain silent about such a game. How long had Lambert been running this? How many victims had there already been? And who had they been? Surely their bodies had been disposed of off the estate, unless Ross had a furnace because he couldn't imagine the man keeping his trophies. Maybe his victims befell some accident miles from here with no trace back to Richton Hall, like Lambert claimed.

Harry shuddered. The room he was in, Lambert Ross's trophy room, was obviously the place where his victims were dissected before their disposal. It was like something from a horror film, yet those films were often inspired by historical and sometimes present day facts. There were many unbelievable atrocities being carried out in the world right now, and this was one of them.

Were any of Lambert Ross's friends participating in the forthcoming devious machinations? And if so, how many? Did they participate in the inevitable dissection like some feverish cult?

Harry laughed out loud at the absurdity.

Most probably the people who would come after him in this sport, as Lambert Kovac called it, would be his own highly skilled security guards.

This whole predicament would sound ludicrous if Harry were not in it himself. There was certainly an abundance of lunatics in the world to whom this sort of thing might be appealing, and Harry had dealt with his fair share of society dregs, but this whole hunter and hunted thing took the proverbial biscuit. This is England, not some dictatorial developing society.

Harry wondered what Parisa would do when she failed to hear from him. Their communication had been regular, as it often is between two people in this age of the smartphone, but there have been times when the messages are less frequent. It's not like they're in each others pockets. But Parisa would likely expect to hear that he is either on his way home or remaining in the village another night. Would she worry? Probably not, because Parisa wasn't a worrier. And yet to not hear anything whatsoever, and with full knowledge of what he had embarked upon, his apparent disappearance might alert her to some danger, especially considering everything else going on at the moment.

Would Parisa come looking for him? Harry hoped not because the last thing he desired was her placed in danger.

That thought alone would propel Harry's actions.

But was it already too late?

By nature Harry wasn't a defeatist and he certainly was not licked yet, far from it, but he suddenly realised with a sinking feeling that this would probably be his last night on earth. Lambert Ross's system must be foolproof for him to have succeeded at it for so many years, and the odds would be stacked heavily against Harry.

Banishing counterproductive negative thoughts from his mind Harry set about a thorough search of the room. He looked for any object which might be used as a weapon, beyond the obvious, or fashioned into one. Harry was going to be an animal which his hunter, or hunters, should not underestimate. Those previously hunted had probably been unsuccessful because of their lateral thinking which meant Harry had to think far beyond the box.

Loosing track of the passing hours while he meticulously inspected every inch of the room and all available tools, Harry barely noticed the sound of a key being turned in the lock to the door which led to the Hall, until Gough was opening it. The butler held a revolver beneath a silver service tray upon which was a plate of steaming vegetables and slices of ham, a dessert bowl with rhubarb crumble and custard, and a pint glass with orange juice.

"Your dinner, sir." Gough announced, like nothing out of the ordinary was occurring. He placed the tray on the bench nearest to him before departing, the lock clicking with an inevitable finality.

Harry shrugged: might as well eat the hearty last meal of the condemned man.

As Harry expected the food was excellent and the orange not from a carton. He was fully sated after the unhurried meal, allowing the nutrients to fully absorb into his system, providing energy for what would be a very long night. If his captors had chosen to drug his food with a substance designed to make him more docile then they would be sorely disappointed. Narcotics failed to have any impact on Harry's metabolism.

While eating, Harry contemplated no further the negative aspects of his situation, for to do so was futile and potentially fatal.

Harry was confident that he probably had a mental and physical edge over those who had come before him, which he would exploit. The weapons he had furnished were rudimentary but workable. He could also set a few traps of his own if he desired, for Harry knew there would be some set for him in the great outdoors.

Closing his eyes Harry pulled the return route through the estate to the village from his memory, mentally plotting his course through the garden and trees, trying to pinpoint where there were raised flower beds and higher rising hedges to offer concealment. He was counting on the predictable nature of humans. Most of his predecessors would undoubtedly have chosen the dense woodland as cover. It offered the better option, at least to the average person. But that was undoubtedly what the hunter, or hunters, would count on. So for Harry the woodland would be used only as a last resort option, a desperate fallback.

Harry was now resigned to letting Lambert Ross's idea of sport commence.

It was gone midnight when Harry heard the sound of metal scraping against wood and brick. It came from the door at the back of the room, the one without the handle. The door itself seemed to vibrate minutely. Then all was silent once more.

Harry gathered up the accoutrements he had found or furnished himself from the bench where he had laid them earlier, placing them about his person in such a way they were easily accessible and didn't hamper his freedom of movement.

Once he had done that, he switched off the light and waited ten minutes until his eyes grew accustomed to the darkness. Harry prided himself on his naturally strong night vision and senses, both of which he hoped would serve him well.

Harry slowly nudged open the outer door an inch at a time, careful to make no noise. As the gap widened he discovered the night sky was clear and there was not too much moonlight. The doorway backed onto a tall hedge, presenting two options to him. Harry had been able to judge that the trophy room was located at the very rear of Richton Hall, and if he chose either left or right as his exit onto the grounds both would present similar challenges. Basically, it didn't really matter where he went. One didn't offer an advantage over the other.

Lambert Ross would have to keep this kind of game quiet, naturally, and maybe only a select few of his employees would take part tonight. No doubt there were a few likeminded fellows more than willing to participate in Lambert's hobbies usually, and these would be his most trusted friends.

Dropping onto all fours, Harry made his way slowly in the right-hand direction between hedge and wall while methodically brushing the ground before placing each hand in front of him as a precaution. One couldn't predict what the floor was covered with, even a thorn in his hand would be an irritation, plus he didn't know how creative Lambert Ross would be.

The grass was slightly damp to the touch. A summer dew. Either that or the vegetation was weeping for him.

Harry reached the open ground. The stars shone brightly. He could make out jagged shadows of sinewy trees, a blotchy canopy of nighttime leaves, blots of flower beds and borders and undefinable man-made structures.

The air was relatively still.

If not for the situation itself, Harry would have enjoyed the evening.

The sounds of midnight included susurration from above, indiscriminate wildlife barks and calls, plus a gentle hum from a generator within Richton Hall. Probably only Harry could detect the last sound because of his attuned senses, but it was certainly present. He had always heard sounds which many people were unaware of, and in fact, during his time with the police, he had solved cases because of that skill.

Something snapped. A twig! A gun safety? The bolt of a crossbow?

Harry held his breath, ears straining, but after a full five minutes there was no other noise.

Slowly, Harry emerged from the pitch darkness across the nighttime lawn where he was aware that he would be visible to anyone watching. Behind him the Hall was an unlit jagged black mass looming ominously. Harry realised the hunters would likely give him a head start, because otherwise where would the fun be?

The grass was soft and dry and Harry made no sound as he walked on all fours to the edge of the woodland. If the hunters had night-vision goggles, which they no doubt would, and they were observing him now, then heading into the large expanse of woodland is something all their previous prey predictably did.

For now he moved fifteen feet into the black mass of trees, laying flat on the ground, partially obscured by the undergrowth. This is where Harry remained for a long ten minutes while he observed the house and open ground which was in darkness, yet any movement would be visible to him.

Harry had another route planned.

The hunter, or hunters, wouldn't want a prolonged chase in case their prey escaped. There might be traps set amongst the trees, or motion-sensing cameras. If nobody had survived before then there must be a few fail safe options at Lambert Ross's disposal.

Edging over the twig- and leaf-strewn ground wasn't the stealthy option because of the noise Harry made, but he was able to cover quite a distance in relatively short time before he reached his target. He was inside the L-shaped corner of the woodland to the right-hand side of the Hall, which the driveway passed through. Harry continued until he reached the leading edge of the trees.

This location offered him a prime view of the front of the Hall, the woodland through which he had been, and the front lawn and garden of the estate. Thanks to the cloudless sky he should be able to see if anyone was moving around the Hall, or positioning themselves in the tree-lined driveway heading toward Richton Village - unless a greetings committee already existed.

How soon would they locate him?

Movement between the hedge where he started and the woodland caught Harry's eye. A black-clad figure, tall, slender and carrying a mini-crossbow, it's metal glinting, prowled across the grass. It wasn't Lambert Ross, that's for sure. This man lacked the politicians rotundness. His eyes were covered by a hi-tech pair of military grade night visions goggles.

Harry was out of range for the goggles to be effective. The clearness of the sky would benefit him more than the hunters. The goggles would have an effectiveness of one-fifty to two hundred yards.

The man was prowling the woodland ten yards from its edge, head turned toward the hidden depths, sweeping and searching, getting nearer and nearer to the corner which Harry had vacated. He silently observed the man's pattern, his gait and the way he loosely held the crossbow.

Harry gritted his teeth impatiently. The man was fifty feet away. There was just the two of them, unless somebody watched from the darkness surrounding the Hall, but Harry doubted this hunt would be that well coordinated.

Onward the man prowled, nearer and nearer, not suspecting that Harry was now positioned a few mere feet behind him.

Harry padded softly to the leading edge of trees, momentarily losing sight of the overconfident hunter, then he bolted around the corner in a burst of speed. The man registered Harry's presence too late, the detective already had one arm about his neck, hand over mouth, while he wenched the man's right arm, the one holding the crossbow, wickedly breaking it at the elbow and yanking the shoulder out of joint.

The man gave a muffled grunt before he passed out.

The crossbow fell on the grass with a thud.

Harry lowered the man to the ground and dragged him into the trees. He patted him down but the man wasn't carrying anything Harry could use, before retrieving the crossbow.

As Harry bent down an immediate high-pitched whistle split the air, lasting for a few seconds, ending with a thud amongst the trees. Harry was knocked off his feet, pain searing his left shoulder.

That had been much too close for comfort.

Without hesitation Harry rolled across the grass to avoid a further shot. He dove into the trees behind the body of the first hunter as another bolt whistled by him, thudding solidly into wood.

Harry scanned the area but couldn't see the shooter, who was too well concealed within the darkness of Richton Hall. His heart raced and the pain to his shoulder was insistent, but it soon subsided to a dull throb.

He cursed his bad luck and stupidity.

With no time to lose Harry wriggled through the undergrowth and gathered a fair distance between himself and the potential assailant before coming to rest. He had sustained more scrapes to add to the bolt but better those irritations than the alternative. His only regret was he couldn't bring with him the crossbow or the downed man's night-vision goggles.

Harry didn't procrastinate.

Standing his full height, getting to the edge of the trees, Harry stared hard into the quarter-light across the estate toward the Hall. Trees lining the driveway resembled sentry-like columns, the dark patches of flowerbeds were undefinable black pools, while the Hall was a terrifying edifice.

Harry hoped he would now be out of effective range of anyone watching.

Without delay, Harry bolted from the woodland across the driveway to the nearest tree. He pressed himself firmly against it. The pain to his shoulder was now nothing more than a numb throb. His adrenaline was up like someone who had consumed an energy drink for its instant burst of sugar and caffeine.

After a five-second wait he bolted along the driveway to the next tree. Still no sign of anyone. How many were out there hunting him?

On his next sprint he decided to move away from direction of the Hall, deeper into the uneven surface of the orchard. He ran fifty feet before dropping to the ground behind a raised flower bed. Looking over its crest he was directly in line with the Hall, some four-hundred feet away.

Now he saw movement. The dark figure of a hunter cautiously moving along the woodland edge toward the Hall, from where Harry had been. He wasn't alone. He was helping the chap whom Harry had earlier encountered and rendered unconscious.

While these two were distracted Harry sprinted a further hundred-feet nearer the perimeter fence, weaving between trees. The only sound was the wind whistling by his ears and a owl screeching from afar. He dodged tree debris and flowerbeds, slipping only once on something unseen.

Which had been fortunate, because not two feet further along the glint and sheen of metal alerted Harry to a spring-loaded track, which he circumvented, coming to rest behind a broad oak tree.

The fence was seventy-five feet in front of him. Latticed with tree branches and other foliage, it disappeared from sight as it swung around eastward in the direction of Richton Village and the original gateway. The distance wasn't immense but being hunted in darkness made it appear further.

Harry looked back at the Hall and across the open ground, which was bathed in a quarter-light nighttime aura of shadows and starry sky. Indistinguishable objects flitted and blurred on the periphery of his eyes, but when Harry looked, straining to see what they were, there was nothing tangible present.

Until movement alerted him.

He froze.

A hunter, this one more rotund, judging from the shadowy form, was prowling the driveway not much more than thirty-feet from Harry. How he had not seen Harry yet was a miracle. This man wore goggles like his companions but maybe the starlight was somehow reducing their effectiveness.

Harry stood stock still. He could feel the blood creeping down his arm from the wound sustained moments ago. He didn't want another.

The man was creeping along as stealthily as he knew, practiced in this form of hunting but with a naive instinct. Harry could see evidence that he was nervous. His steps were too cautious, too tentative, and clearly he lacked the confidence which Lambert Ross required right now.

This new man wasn't a trained security guard. Maybe he was a close friend of the politician.

Harry didn't hesitate. This time there was nobody else watching. When the man was just ten-feet away Harry lurched forward, tripped the man who went sprawling, dropping the crossbow. Harry pressed the man's face into the grass and didn't release the pressure until he was certain the man was very much dead.

Anger and determination coursed through his very psyche.

Harry picked up the crossbow. He also checked the man's pockets, and ear for a Bluetooth device, but there was nothing of use. He waited and watched for a good fifteen minutes. Harry had already done admirably to get this far, he didn't want to ruin his luck. Dawn wouldn't be upon him for a few more hours. The hunters, however many remained, would get more frustrated the nearer it got to daylight. Would Lambert Ross now be feeling this game with Harry was a bad idea? Harry doubted anyone had come close to the success which he was experiencing. Maybe as the hours ticked by, Lambert and his hunters would become more desperate or use better technology to locate him.

The trick would be to not allow them time.

Harry ran more cautiously, more methodically, now. The trees were dense and spindly, while the flowerbeds and patches of vegetables had better borders. It was easier for Harry to get within twenty-feet of the fence.

He would have to be careful of the inevitable surveillance cameras now.

There were no telltale indications of hidden cameras or the glint of infrared lights to detect motion. If audio sensors were present there was nothing Harry could do about those except to be very quiet indeed.

After five minutes waiting and watching and listening, Harry crawled upon all fours like some nocturnal creature. Stealthily he moved, metre by metre, tasting the low lying air and feeling the soft grass on the palm of his hands.

Sharp pain burst through his wounded shoulder, causing him to stumble and drop to his knees to relieve the burning pressure to his arm. Harry cursed inwardly. The niggling numb sensation of bruised nerves and severed skin, blood trickling down his arm, reminded him how lucky he had been so far. He tried shaking the pain out, breathing deeply. It got better. The crawling had obviously caused his injury to flair up.

The solid remains of the gateway to Richton Village was not more than two-hundred yards away. There was no manmade light beyond. Lovely and dark and quaint for its residents.

Harry neared the gate, stopping fifty-yards from it, crouching low against the shrubbery.

Reaching this far now seemed relatively easy. The hunters who remained in pursuit had either underestimated him terribly or they had all gathered resolutely beyond this point, because this was Harry's only means of exiting the estate grounds. The gateway through the village. He didn't expect to find his car. They had something planned for that. Maybe it had been driven far away and burnt out, like he'd been in an accident.

Harry shuddered at the thought of the soul sacrificed for Lambert Ross's hideous game, the body which was to be found in his car, his own undiscovered.

All the more reason to succeed.

He checked the crossbow. It had a revolving cartridge of twelve bolts, all of which were present. The safety was on. Harry squeezed the trigger using the index finger from his injured arm. The pain was bearable. He considered discarding the makeshift weapons he had fashioned in the trophy room, none had as yet been necessary, but that would be tempting fate.

Crouching as low as he could, Harry silently, slowly, edged across the garden to toward the gateway, its imposing arch seeming to bear down oppressively the nearer he got to it.

Harry's eyes were wide and staring as he scoured the nighttime darkness for telltale signs of movement.

He saw the outline of a person against the side wall of the nearest building and slowly dropped to the ground behind the gateway. No sudden movement to attract attention.

Had the person seen him?

Whoever awaited him, and however many, these would be Ross's security personnel. They would be fully trained professionals.

Which meant Harry couldn't be sloppy in his approach.

He cautiously peered through an opening in the brick gateway and saw the person hadn't moved. There was the faintest blue dot of light at the persons head, meaning this security detail were in communication with one another. If Harry could successfully take out this guy and get his Bluetooth device, that would be an immense bonus.

Judging the distance, Harry gently flicked off the crossbows safety catch. Taking aim, his arm remarkably steady, Harry slowly squeezed the trigger and the weapon shuddered imperceptibly as the bolt was loosed.

Harry didn't witness the result, but certainly heard the thud of the bolt striking concrete and the subsequent dropping of a body onto the ground. Clearly the bolt had passed right through the person and hit the wall behind him. A satisfying result for Harry. One down, who knew how many remaining.

Leaving the safety off the crossbow, Harry padded forward on the balls of his feet, crouching at intervals, as he made his way to the body on the floor. He met no resistance and was thankful nobody else was observing this area.

Harry removed the Bluetooth device from the dead man's ear, wiped it clean, and put it into his own. He heard some chatter, innocuous banter, nothing helpful to Harry yet. He also removed the man's night vision goggles and put them on, adjusting them to suit his own eyes.

His hopes and heart rose.

Via the Bluetooth Harry could hear chattering from Ross's people as they fed constant reports about their positions. Their help will benefit him, but it wouldn't be too long before they realised one of their own was missing. He could at least avoid them, and the sooner Harry departed the village the better because he was starting to feel slightly lightheaded through loss of blood from the shoulder injury, and probably exhaustion from the long night.

Harry moved through the broken darkness along a narrow footpath behind the residences and cafe, soon reaching the perimeter of the car park, which was empty.

Evidently Ross's men had already disposed of his car. Harry clenched his teeth. Parisa would be frantic having not heard from him for hours, and if Ross had crashed and burned Harry's car, as he knew was likely the case, Parisa would believe him dead.

He circled the car park on the wrong side of the fence, scratching and stinging himself on the shrubbery, without catching sight of any of Ross's people. They were concentrating their efforts near the church and along the street, judging by the chatter, and it wasn't until Harry reached the exit road that he saw one of them perched in a wooden bird hide halfway up an oak tree.

The night vision goggles were a blessing for Harry. It was fortunate he had seen the spotter first. He was able to burrow through the base of a hedgerow and work his way onto the main road from the village without being seen.

Harry found an opening into a field and walked through it parallel with the road, out of sight.

A car trundled by, it's lights on full. Lambert Ross was obviously becoming very desperate.

It took Harry a good ninety-minutes to reach the outskirts of Bramfield. The trudge along uneven ground and unfamiliar terrain had been exhausting, and he collapsed on the verge, where he lay for five minutes, the goggles slipping off his head.

Harry could barely think. He knew what he needed to do. He knew The Red Stag Inn couldn't be too far now. But did he have the energy to reach it?

# CHAPTER TWENTY-SIX

Harry awoke with a stinging discomfort crawling across his skin and the softness of a top sheet above him. Sunshine blazed beyond his red eyelids, streaming through a window but he screwed his eyes tightly against it. He turned his head away. His neck felt tight and he realised a bandage encased his shoulder where the crossbow bolt had penetrated, but there was no pain.

Expecting to see the interior of a hospital room when he opened his eyes he was taken aback to discover he was in the bedroom of a woman. The decor was unmistakably feminine with its egg-shell blue and pastel yellow painted walls, pink flowery bedspread turned down, and various accoutrements on the bedside cabinet. There was no clock to be seen but judging from the angle of the suns rays streaming through the window it was approaching noon.

Harry could hear crockery being moved in a distant kitchen. A coffee machine was emitting steam.

Using his good arm Harry was able to lever himself up to a more comfortable sitting position. He ached and itched and the smell of ointment was strong in the air. Harry was naked under the sheet and his body was blotchy with red abrasions, sporadic bruising and there were clusters of small pink bumps where he had come into contact with stinging nettles. The bandage about his shoulder was professionally applied, the wound a dull numbing throb now that he was upright.

Harry wondered how much blood he had lost and why he wasn't in a hospital bed? The last thing he remembered was passing out before reaching the car park of The Red Stag Inn in Bramfield.

At least he was no longer in danger unless this was a gilded cage, which did not seem to be the case.

Harry would find out soon enough who his saviour was because the stairs creaked as someone ascended them. The footfalls were light, belonging to a person of small stature. He could smell the deliciously strong coffee before it arrived, and his stomach grumbled in response.

"Good morning, Harry."

Much to Harry's surprise his host was the nurse from The Red Stag Inn, whose husband had been the reporter she claimed had perished because he had dug into Lambert Ross's life to his detriment. And with that recollection Harry realised he might know how her husband had died?

"Rosita?" Harry said.

The nurses eyes lit up with delight that he had remembered her name.

"That's good," she replied, "at least you don't have a concussion."

Harry let out a small laugh.

"I made an impression, then?" Rosita said, handing him a bowl of cereal while placing the coffee on the bedside cabinet. "How do you feel?"

"Better than I might've done." Harry ate a spoonful of milky granola. "Thank you, although..."

"You're welcome. I found you when I was on my way to work this morning, and remembered what you said about being a private investigator. I presume you visited Lambert Ross at his estate yesterday."

"Yes, but..."

"I had a hunch you wouldn't want to be taken to a hospital in case Ross's people found out you were there. I presume the shoulder wound is their work?"

Harry nodded, "That's very astute of you."

Rosita sat at the foot of the bed, silently watching Harry as he ate more of the granola. He was very hungry and thirsty after his long night but he also had lots of questions for her. The bowl was soon emptied. He swapped it with the mug of coffee.

"Can I use use your phone?" Harry asked.

Rosita handed it to him without hesitation and Harry dialled the number of Parisa's mobile phone. She practically screamed down the line with delight to hear his voice because, as he had suspected, his car had met a fiery grave on a road between Hertford and Norfolk. Harry quickly explained to Parisa what had really happened before asking her to meet him in Bramfield and to please bring him a change of clothes He was reluctant to hanging up because it was a relief to hear her voice, but he had many other things to attend to.

Next Harry phoned the police, told them who he was and briefly explained what had happened. They would be sending someone over immediately.

"Do you think I'm some drunken crazy woman?" Rosita asked when Harry handed back her phone. "For believing my husband was murdered by Lambert Ross for prying into his life, I mean?"

Harry laughed gently, "Not now I've experienced the world of Lambert Ross firsthand, I must admit."

"And you think my husband might have been onto something?"

"Hmm, in all likelihood he was, Rosita." He replied at length. "There are many things which Ross is doing on that estate of his. The police will be very interested to hear what I have to tell them, I can guarantee that. Hopefully they will also take a greater interest in your husbands death. I just hope they don't take too long getting here."

Harry figured that Lambert Ross would have a fairly efficient clean-up operation following Harry's escape. "Look...if your husband was indeed murdered...then I have a feeling I know how Ross accomplished it."

Rosita's eyes lit up with obvious satisfaction mixed with the moisture of tears. Clearly her persistence and patience since her husband's death had some vilification thanks to the encouragement of Harry's words. But the politician was canny. No doubt he would have plenty of well thought out plans in place should anyone try to expose his game. Now that Harry thought back to his personal success, he knew it was imperative the police wasted little time getting here before Lambert Ross and his team could erase all evidence of what transpired last night.

"Would you..." Rosita said, wiping tears from her relief-filled eyes, "would you like to see the handwritten notes my husband kept? He was quite old-fashioned really, bless him. He didn't trust computers."

"Very much so." Harry replied. "And I wouldn't mind getting out of bed, if that's okay?"

Rosita laughed, "Yes, of course. Your clothes are on my line. They should be dry by now. I'll get them."

"Thank you."

Thirty minutes later Harry Kovac had showered, dressed, and was seated at the breakfast bar in Rosita's kitchen with a second mug of strong black coffee. He couldn't thank her enough for the kindness she was showing him, but Rosita brushed off the compliment.

"I'm a nurse," she stated, "it's what I do."

"All the same..."

"If you expose Ross's viciousness, then that will be enough thanks. I hope those are helpful?"

Harry had in front of him a thick folder of handwritten A4 sheets of paper. These were the notes which Rosita's husband had made about Lambert Ross, which she had astutely hidden because, she claimed, her home had been covertly searched by the politicians security detail shortly after the death of her husband.

The writing was in block capitals, relatively legible, and Harry had barely scratched the surface of the details when a knock came upon the front door.

Rosita show in two police officers who were from the local constabulary, which transpired was the Hertford station.

After the introductions - Detective's O'Rietty and Toterro - Harry gave a succinct yet detailed report of what occurred last night to the two detectives from CID. Inwardly, Harry wished they were from his own branch, because like many police officers these two were politely yet cynically assessing the information rather than taking Harry's words at face value.

"You can appreciate the need to get to Richton with reasonable alacrity," Harry concluded. "No doubt Lambert Ross is erasing signs of my incarceration and escape quite efficiently and wiping away any trace of evidence. It will be problematic for him to remove the damage caused to his property, though."

"What do you suggest we do, Mister Kovac?" Detective O'Rietty, the taller, stockier of the two, asked.

"I know the protocol," Harry said to the stoic face that asked the question, trying not to let frustration get the better of him. Harry had been in their shoes many times. "I realise we can't go stomping in without probable cause, but Richton Village is open to all visitors. They can't turn us away. I can retrace my steps and hopefully find something which incriminates Ross and his people, something which backs up my claim." He looked from one to the other. "And then there's my burned out car. I'm sure forensics can soon see that it wasn't my body which was inside."

Detective O'Rietty nodded thoughtfully. 'I won't patronise you, Mister Kovac. I can tell you're a good detective. Past and present. And as you are aware a case has to be built up with substantial evidence before arrests can be made, etcetera." The detective gesticulated and paced around the kitchen a lot. "Your testimony is very compelling, that's a big advantage. You have a wound on your shoulder from a crossbow bolt. Your car was found burned out in a field between here and your home. Now we are going to take a friendly reconnaissance of the land owned by the perpetrator of all these events you claim happened, where we hope to find some evidence that corroborates your story and places you at Richton Hall, and that this game took place. But even with all these details attached to your story, if the esteemed politician Mister Lambert Ross has wiped the place clean and fixed a solid alibi for himself, then we are faced with the possibility that Mister Ross would bring charges against you for defamation of character."

Rosita snorted with derision. "Typical! This is the same treatment I received when my husband was murdered by Ross."

"Standard operational procedures," Harry said, "I'm sorry to say."

"He was murdered?" Detective Totorro raised a quizzical eyebrow.

Harry raised a hand to silence the fiery Rosita, which surprisingly had the desired effect.

Detective O'Rietty hadn't said anything which Harry hadn't already considered himself. Despite everything he had gone through and witnessed firsthand, he realised all too well that if no concrete evidence was presented then Ross would walk Scott free from any allegation lain at his feet. Many hours had passed since Harry's incarceration and the politicians spin-doctors could easily have worked their magic.

"There's no more time to waste," Harry told Detective O'Rietty decisively, then to Rosita he said, "My friend Parisa Dane will arrive soon. Are you okay to stay here with her until we return?"

"Of course."

"Thank you, sincerely, for everything."

# CHAPTER TWENTY-SEVEN

Detective O'Rietty parked the unmarked police car in the quarter-full Richton Village pay and display area, but instead of getting a ticket, he placed the convenient police parking pass on the dashboard which permitted such a privilege as not paying.

Harry led the way, retracing his steps around the perimeter of the car park and along the side of the field and overgrown hedgerow behind the buildings, indicating his route to them. He expected to find nothing here because he hadn't left incriminating evidence of his presence, not even the bolt of a crossbow. Presumably any substantial damage to buildings or trees couldn't be repaired, and maybe there would be DNA belonging to himself or one of Ross's hunters.

When they emerged from the footpath and passed through the gateway they were given nothing but a cursory glance from a gardener. Everything appeared normal on the surface. And why wouldn't it? If a cleanup operation had been thorough then Ross's people would have been briefed on what to expect today. Harry wondered if the gardener they saw had been present during last nights hunt.

Harry shuddered inwardly. He wasn't normally shaken by mankind's atrocities, but the thought that the politician had disposed of the bodies of his own security guards in the manner intended for Harry, sickened him.

"I incapacitated at least two of Ross's people." Harry stated. "It would be good if I could chat with the man himself. Or Gough, his butler."

"Probable cause, Mister Kovac." Detective Totorro prompted, an unnecessary reminder that Harry would be getting himself into trouble if he used intimidation against Ross or any of his people.

The law of the land had Harry tied up in red tape and knots. He knew he was damned if he went in like a bull in the proverbial China shop, despite his desire for retribution. Harry was tired and couldn't afford to let the lack of sleep get the better of his senses of reason and logic. He angrily ground his teeth.

They plodded onward for a further five minutes until Harry knew how futile their search was.

"Fuck it!" Harry seethed uncharacteristically, but the situation had gotten the better of him, his anger and exhaustion spent. "Let's go. I'm wasting your time! This is hopeless. We aren't going to find anything. Lambert Ross is too canny to leave anything to chance. Let's face it, he has got away with this sport of his to long and nothing has been done about it for a reason. This is his land, his estate, his life! Any mess has been efficiently destroyed. So be it, I've got to find concrete proof by some other means."

The two detectives couldn't disagree, and they said nothing by way of response, simply putting on the best sympathetic faces.

Back at Rosita's cottage in Bramfield, Parisa had arrived and cried tears of relief when reunited with Harry - he, normally emotionally well poised, had to tense his jaw to prevent his own tears from prevailing. He was equally relieved to see her, pleased to be alive, frustrated that his quarry was likely to get away with his game…for now, at least. Harry was tired and angry and had set his mind toward determinedly seeing to it that Lambert Ross received his comeuppance, whenever that time arrived.

Parisa hugged him to her and despite the pain across his body Harry didn't want to release her. Their moment was fleetingly brief as dictated by their location, but it would not be their last, and yet it was difficult to bring an end too it.

The two detectives had gone their merry way, case, if not permanently closed, then put on hold. There was still the investigation into Harry's burnt out car to be resolved.

"Thank you for everything." Harry said with gratitude to Rosita.

"You're welcome." Rosita's voice was filled with the resignation that Harry was now leaving, with the unresolved issue of her husbands death attached to the departure. "Not than I'm putting down my own work, but you really do need to go to a hospital to have your shoulder checked out."

Harry nodded, "I know how important your husbands notes are to you, Rosita, but if there's anything buried within them that I might be able to use against Lambert Ross, I shall need to temporarily borrow them."

"That's fine." Rosita said.

After saying their farewells, with a promise to keep Rosita abreast of any revelations, they departed Bramfield for home, with Parisa driving. Harry filled her in with all the events which occurred to him at Richton Hall and the estate, trying his best to make light the elements of danger.

Harry dozed off thanks to the soothing motion of the car, lack of sleep and his injuries, and he didn't wake until Parisa was parking up at Norfolk and Norwich University Hospital's A&E entrance. Despite champing at the bit to get back to the office, Harry permitted his arm to be assessed, the bandage to be changed, a blood test carried out, and for Parisa to supply him with much needed coffee and a sandwich.

"I hope you don't mind me mothering you?" Parisa asked when they were back in her car.

"Not at all."

"After all…I did think you were dead."

"I understand," he told her, squeezing her hand in reassurance as they kissed. "The good news is I'm not entirely incapacitated!" He added with a sly grin.

"I shall hold you to that."

They immediately drove to the offices of Crane & Associates Investigation Services, where the reassuring sight of Daphne Crane's smiling yet wane face greeted them. Teri Hamilton leant casually against the coffee machine, all professionalism, having been contacted by Daphne regarding the return of Harry. Both were relieved to see him in reasonable shape.

"It's been a busy day or two." Harry said flippantly, lowering himself painfully into one of the office chairs.

"That's an understatement." Daphne said. "So what's happened to you, Harry?"

Harry filled them all in on his visit to Bramfield, Richton Village and the estate, detailing Lambert Ross's idea of sport omitting not a single fact.

"You're lucky to be alive." Daphne stated.

Parisa had averted her face, she was crying.

"I have this young woman Rosita's dead husbands notes to go through," Harry concluded. "Seems he was a reporter investigating Lambert Ross and got murdered - Rosita's claim - for his efforts. If there's something juicy in this paperwork, and I'm hoping there is, then it might just be enough to utterly discredit Ross and end his political ambitions once and for all."

Daphne snorted derisively, "Because his son murdering Zero isn't nearly enough for the police!"

Harry nodded, "Hmm, it would seem so, at least at the moment. But Lambert Ross's real self will be exposed soon enough, I'm sure of it. It's inevitable that this construct, his fake media persona will finally bend and bow and collapse. And it is a construct, albeit one professionally honed. But let's face it, we all put on different personas for different areas of our life and sometimes they crumble. Doesn't matter who you are."

"True." Teri concurred.

"Anyway," Harry said to Teri, "what's happening with car thing?"

"Car thing!?" Parisa said.

"I know, it's a famous one."

Teri laughed, "So famous that we opened up a can of worms and now the predators have come to feed."

Harry raised a curious eyebrow.

"Basically it's done and done." Daphne explained.

"Is that so?" Harry asked.

Teri nodded, "Your French friend JP dug up some information on the name Adam Richardson, for us. Apparently it's a fake name. A combination of two significant technicians in the world of the cultural phenomenon which is James Bond. Ken Adam was a set designer, or production designer to give his professional title. He was responsible for much of the spectacular visual stuff which is seen on screen that the franchise is famous for. John Richardson was what's known as a Special Effects Supervisor. He would create and blow up miniatures of full sized objects, things like that. Both were exceptionally talented guys, if movies are your thing or not.

"Daphne ran this fake name amalgamate through the computer and the results were…ridiculous."

"Tens of thousands." Daphne sighed.

Harry asked, "I presume they had something to do with the creation of the car we're after?"

"I guess so." Daphne said with a shrug of her shoulders.

"If not," Teri said, "they're both big in the world of James Bond."

"Interesting."

"Believe it or not," Parisa added, "I've got a design book by Ken Adam. Most of his work isn't useable for real life property design, but his imagination was terrific and inspirational to many a flamboyant interior designer."

"So," Harry said, bringing the conversation back to the point, "this Adam Richardson is a cover name for someone else."

Teri gave a sideways tilt of her head, "Sort of. After sifting through the thousands of names, and using the age old process of elimination, we discovered Adam Richardson was a corporate car dealer in Dubai, at least the warehouse at Drydocks World is."

"Drydocks World?" Harry queried.

"Not to be confused with Disney!" Teri quipped. "Anyway, this dealer is relatively small fry but its owners are significantly large fry. Two billionaire Arab brothers responsible for much of the commercial modernisation of the eastern quarter of Dubai, including hospitality and business."

"Let me guess," Harry said, "the film business?" Teri nodded. "And these brothers desired the Bond car so they had it pilfered?"

"Not exactly." Teri said. "They bought it legitimately off the person who did have it stolen."

Harry scratched his temple. "I don't want to sound flippant, but you seem have dug all this up very easily considering how long professional hunters have been trying to locate it."

"What are trying to to say!" Daphne laughed.

"Nothing personal."

"You remember the guy who came to our office warning you off the hunt?" Teri prompted.

"Sure."

"It seems he was working for the people who actually found it." Teri explained. "But due to the politically sensitive nature of its ownership they realised we might expose the persons involved, so filled us in on a few of the less secret details."

"The basic facts behind the discovery of the Aston Martin were released to the media with relatively little fanfair last night." Daphne added. "It seems this is news too old for anyone other than fans of James Bond to care about."

"Basically what you're saying is," Harry said, "Stephen Smith's folly was a waste of our time and his money."

Teri and Daphne nodded simultaneously.

Harry laughed. Smith and Climmy wouldn't be getting their fortune and glory after all.

Harry sat alone in his office, door closed, an hour after the others had departed. Parisa would return for him at five o'clock. Dinner, wine, and more, at hers.

Earbuds in, Harry sifted through the paper work which he had brought with him from Bramfield, trying to find the one thing which might have caused Rosita's husband to be silenced by Lambert Ross.

After lots of nothing, hours of nothing, it was finally presented itself like a beacon. The wheat amongst the chaff.

A leak from the Official Secrets Act. Do not open until the year 2045.

Explosive if it was genuine.

But was it enough for the public to be in uproar? Was it enough of a scandal, enough of a military cover-up, to provoke reassessment of the politician? Arguably much worse had transpired in this age of total surveillance and total exposure, yet this was different. It was the military hierarchy covering a heinous crime to save face.

Harry read, absorbed the details:

Lambert Ross had been privately condemned for obeying dubious orders from a subsequently dishonoured officer. On the sixth of May, 1982, at sixteen-hundred hours plus five, while serving in the army during the Falklands War, Lambert had been asked to kill in cold blood four American soldiers who had been fighting for the Argentinian Army. This quartet were chosen for execution instead of interning them as prisoners of war for later military trial. To save face. Young Ross's officer had ordered two men prior to Lambert to carry it out. Both had refused. Lambert did not hesitate, emotionlessly executing the four soldiers, secretly taking pleasure from doing so.

There had been no witnesses, with only the officer sharing in this secret, but during a subsequent investigation into the event by a closed military trial Lambert Ross chose an honourable discharge from the service. The officer in charge received early retirement. Naturally the military didn't want this heinous crime publicly exposed, so the report and trial was buried amongst the Official Secrets Act.

This embarrassment alone might be enough to disgrace Lambert Ross MP, but apparently Rosita's husband had discovered Ross later befriended his old officer. Nothing wrong with that, of course. They had much in common. But it wasn't more than five years after the end of the Falklands War that the officer died in a car crash. Brake failure. A freak accident. Nothing untoward was discovered or reported. Case closed.

Harry leant back in his office chair. Had the same fate befell Ross's senior officer that had befallen Rosita's husband? That was to have been Harry's fate?

The answer in Harry's mind was a resounding yes.

But there was no proof. No facts. So there was nothing he could do with that particular information. The Falklands execution on the other hand…

Harry composed an email addressed to Begona Lec, detailing the salient points. His reporter friend would be extremely interested in this leaked military secret, which might be enough to bury Lambert Ross's career once and for all.

## CHAPTER TWENTY-EIGHT

Lambert Ross stood at the impromptu pedestal erected in front of the lawns at Richton Hall, presenting a lovely countryside view to those watching his televised address, clear morning skies adding to the picturesque backdrop. The politician looked tired but was otherwise his usual arrogant braggart self.

"There have been many unsubstantiated claims made against me since I announced my return to the political arena." He began, expression stern, tone serious. "There have been old stories dragged up from the gutter to service opposition propaganda. This is the cultural makeup we live in and ultimately I must accept this." Lambert Ross paused, the cameras catching his tremulous emotional turmoil for posterity: "New facts which abound regarding my son Winston have recently come to light, and they do not shine a positive light upon his family. I have offered all my resources to aid the authorities as best I can, and I shall address all these claims in due course but the needs of the English population, my people, presently outweigh my own needs. I don't require a law banning me from lying before election time which a neighbouring country has instigated,"

Lambert smiled, his reference causing a ripple of laughter from the fifty journalists gathered unseen behind the camera. They could pry all the like after he had delivered his speech, Ross thought to himself. For now he would answer those as yet unasked questions.

"That law by our neighbour in itself is amusing to me, and needs severe assessment by our own present government. It's an admission that politicians cannot be trusted, or believed, giving vilification to the facts which our citizens are already aware. It goes to show exactly how many blustering old fools there in power right now!

"I don't want to watch the country burn like my opponents claim I do. I am not the same man I was one, five, ten, twenty years ago. I don't want to force us into a civil war by taking a backward into our Empirical past. I want progression, not regression. For years both the major political parties have dug us deeper into debt, tried erasing our historical identity and have allowed our countries infrastructure to be destabilised through immigration. These are the challenges facing any new Government but we need a new government, we need a new direction, which is why I am putting myself in the running for the leadership of Generation You. If I get voted into this establishment then my decision is supported by my country, by the people of my country, and I shall be grateful and thankful and do my best for those people. If, after everything which has transpired in the past few days makes people feel I'm not a worthy potential candidate for Prime Minister of England, than I shall accept your decision with the proper humility."

The picture cut to the presenter in the television studio, who added further context and images pertaining to elements of Lambert Ross's speech. The ticker-tape footer on the screen fed news about Ross's Falklands War service and the allegations against him.

Parisa muted the volume.

Harry Kovac contemplatively watched the politicians televised speech from the sofa in Parisa's lounge, her hand in his, the dull throb to his shoulder a reminder of what Lambert Ross was truly capable. He was grinding his teeth through frustration. Harry of all people knew the slippery slope of political philosophy. He knew

Lambert wouldn't be thrown under the bus by his rich and powerful colleagues. But maybe his reporter friend Begona Lec had set a small cat amongst the pigeons by leaking the official report from almost forty years ago. Perhaps it would have some bearing on public perception of the politician. Or had people become weary of such scandals? Were they bored by what they heard next? Another day, another media figure's revelation!

Permanence is an illusion.

"He's building bridges to preemptively attack those who want to see him fall." Harry said. "That's for sure."

"You did your bit." Parisa offered, sensing Harry's frustration. "And maybe one of the bridges he builds will be wooden over a volcano."

Harry nodded. The outcome wasn't conclusive. Not yet. Harry had done his bit for justice, for law, for right. Call it what you will.

"Speaking which." Parisa said with a cheeky grin, and stood, slipping out of the towel and straddling Harry's lap. He wasn't about to protest.

Authors Notes are available by contacting p.starling@sky.com because there's much to discuss.

# Novels by Paul R Starling

**The Scott Dalton Series**

Living in the Edge - 20th Anniversary Edition
Danger on the Edge
Over the Edge of the Abyss
British Bulldog

Cause and Effect
Life in the Shadows
An Amazing Autobiography

**The Harry Kovac Thrillers**

Blackheart
Cry Havoc
(Harry will return…whether you like it or not!)

Available from Amazon, all good bookshops, or signed from the author by contacting me at p.starling.sky.com

Printed in Great Britain
by Amazon